MISTS OF THE BLUE RIDGE

By Tecla Emerson

Cover Design by Katharine Sodergreen
Sodergreen@aol.com

Interior layout by
Robert Louis Henry
http://leafgardenpress.com

OutLook Press
210 Legion Ave. #6805,
Annapolis, MD 21401
TeclaM@aol.com

~ To Penelope ~

who turned childhood into an adventure

~ INTRODUCTION ~

Olivia had little knowledge and no interest in the makings of a war. Regardless of how she felt, she was called on to make more than her fair share of decisions. Decisions that would not only affect her, but her family and those around her. Olivia was thrown into the middle of the great Civil War.

Abraham Lincoln, the great orator of that time had said: "...*you can not fail, if you resolutely determine, that you will not.*"

It was 1863. This is the story of Olivia and how her determination kept her from failing.

~ CHAPTER ONE ~

They were so close. They were chasing me. Their feet were pounding. I could hear their strangled breathing. I ran, ran as fast as I'd ever run.

Their breath was hot; it felt like burning coals searing the back of my neck. Turning, I looked to see how close they had come – the blue uniforms were gaining. Their faces were hard with huge eyes of a fierce red; fire shot out of their mouths, their knuckles white as they pointed their guns. They were pointed at me. My skirt tangled, it wrapped around my ankles pulling me down. "No, don't fall," I screamed. Yanking hard, I tried to unwrap the fabric, but it only twisted more tightly. I was struck dumb, words strangled in my throat. The nearest one grabbed me.

"Olivia, Olivia, wake up." Someone was pulling on my arm, pulling it nearly out of its socket. My eyes unstuck and flew open. It took a moment to think of where I was and who this was leaning over me.

"You're having a dream," said Ryan, a worry line creased his forehead, "and it must've been wild 'cause you're a mess."

I couldn't move. I stared up at him waiting for my mind to clear. Everything felt damp, my hair was stuck to my face and the flannel of my night dress felt as though it had been plastered to me like a too tight, wrinkly second skin.

"Are you all right?" he asked. My eyes tried to focus. The outline of the room was barely visible in the early morning light. "You're not sick are you? Should I tell Mother?"

"No, leave me be," my voice croaked, sounding rusty. The vision of the nightmare began to fade as I rubbed at my eyes. Wiggling free of the quilt, I tried to swing my legs out of the bed but my nightdress was tangled all around me. Ryan stood a moment looking down at me, a questioning look; he rubbed at what looked like a fresh cut on his chin. There were questions that he had, but he turned and stomped off, his over-sized boots making far too much noise. I shook my head to be rid of the terrors.

"You're going to be late for breakfast," he shot over his shoulder. A trail of the scent of Father's shaving soap followed him – he'd been in his stuff again. You're ten I wanted to say, there's not even peach fuzz on your cheeks, but my tongue wouldn't form the words.

My feet touched the cold floorboards. It had a steadying effect for the wooziness going on in my head. What had I been dreaming? Rarely did I have nightmares; it must have been that extra piece of mutton from last night's dinner that gave me a fitful sleep. Already the image was fading of those blue Yankee uniforms chasing me. I shivered. If they had really caught me, what would I have done? Where were Mother and Father while this was happening? Why was I alone? I shook my head "go way bad dream, go way." I shook my head again just like Nanny Anna had always told us to do when we were little. I did it some more just for good measure "go way bad dream, go way," hoping that it would never again come back to haunt me. Nanny Anna's words prickled at the edge of my mind, the words that dreams foretold the future. I shook my head again for good measure.

Every bone was stiff and creaky making it hard to dress and pull a brush through my hair. I tried to smooth it back and tie it with a ribbon but it was nearly hopeless with all the escaping loose ends. I was going to be late going down, there was no question about that, but I didn't care.

Thankfully, for once breakfast was going to be informal. No one was going to feel much like sitting this morning. I slipped down the stairs and had already taken my seat when Ryan and Molly arrived letting the door bang shut behind them. Each had telltale puffy eyes. Ryan had an annoyed look but chose to keep whatever complaint he had to himself. He stared at me as he took his seat, maybe waiting for me to say something about my bad dream, but I ignored him.

Nanny Anna had left us to pour our own tea and eat a biscuit. This was completely against Mother's rules of formality but every now and again she seemed to lack the energy to get after us. I loved it, this informality with no one talking and not even looking at each other. Eating a second biscuit, I left a trail of crumbs between the buffet and the table. Ryan and Molly ate little and were gone without even excusing themselves.

It was all right. I wanted to think my own thoughts without those two staring at me. My mind tried to settle on good things, like how this morning I didn't have to answer for my appearance. Mother did not tolerate carelessness in dress or one's morning toilet. One did not appear at the breakfast table with anything less than neatly plaited hair and freshly scrubbed faces. This morning was an exception however, and I doubted, had she been here, that she would have even noticed my laziness. She had other, bigger things on her mind. I brushed the crumbs from my lap and left the table to join the rest of the family.

· · ·

~ CHAPTER TWO ~

We were at war.

Andrew tugged on his gray jacket. "Leave go of me Mother," he said. "I'm not a child." The other two were already there; as always, I was the laggard. I took my place along the edge of the veranda. We stood in line like a group of newly recruited soldiers.

"But you are my child," she answered as she straightened his collar. "You always will be no matter if you're 17 or 70." Mother could be like that, she liked to put things in their rightful place. Exasperation flitted across Andrew's face.

"I've got to get a move on or I'll never get there." It was as if we'd never existed for all the attention he gave us.

We stood, holding our breath, lined up in a perfectly straight line. Mother had a tight look around her eyes; her lips were in a thin line struggling to make her face smile. Ryan had his predictable *I don't care* look and Molly looked for all the world as though she were about to jump out of her skin. I stood statue-like except to try to flick the piece of jam stuck to the bodice of my dress.

As I watched him, I'm sure the annoyance was stamped on my frown. Last night's dream aside, which still poked around at the edges of my mind, I had to ask why was he allowed to leave and I wasn't? My life was rushing away before my eyes: I would spend the rest of my days on this horrid farm being part of a moving mass of wool and endless lamb chops, living far from anything that had any meaning or was of any importance.

Andrew jumped down from the veranda choosing the shortcut and not the grand staircase. "Well, you just go on back up there and kiss your momma and sisters," said Father. "A Confederate uniform is no excuse for forgetting your manners."

Their grey eyes met. A look passed between

them that I couldn't understand. Andrew had been his favorite. He'd been working with him all these years to have him take over the farm – now I wondered what would become of all of it in his absence and was Father worried about what would happen.

We lived in Maryland right next to the line where Kanawha or West Virginia as it was now called, had split off. We were just north of the line that had divided off the new state separating it from the old, but our farm was on the west side of the mountain. We were so close to the border of the new state, but we were Marylanders through and through. There was a war going on and our sympathies lay with the south. I think.

It was so confusing, it was hard to even discuss. We had slaves but so did just about everyone that we knew. Andrew and Father seemed to not agree on much of anything having to do with the right and the wrong of things and now here he was heading off to fight for the Confederacy. Father was not happy and it was anyone's guess as to exactly why.

Andrew gave a great sigh then turned and came up the stairs, his long legs taking two at a time. He went down the line and planted a quick kiss on our cheeks, except Ryan that is, who couldn't have been less interested. Molly threw her arms around his neck for a brief moment. Andrew at seventeen had never paid much attention to the two youngest. I was his favorite, there was no doubt about that. We were closest in age, me being sixteen and he just one year older. We exchanged a knowing look and he bent and whispered, "Take care of them," before turning quickly and giving Mother one more of the required kisses. Mother tried to stand tall and proud but I saw her shudder as though an icicle had slid down her back.

"Good bye, Sir," he said to Father. Father hesitated for just a moment before shaking the young hand extended to him. We remained like cold marble statues as Elijah flicked the reins on the two chestnut geldings. "Ee up," he said. Father turned away not even waiting 'til they made it to the end of the drive. His uneven footsteps led back to the house. He let the door slam behind him. Mother was dabbing at her tears. She was so pale her skin was the color of one of our ghostly morning fogs. Her chest heaved in silence as she tried to hold back the sobs that were tucked somewhere down deep, threatening to erupt.

"Why is he doing this?" asked Ryan, his fingers playing with the shirttail that should have been tucked in. How could he ask that? How many times had we been over it?

"And where were you last night? Were you not at the table having dinner with all of us?" I asked.

"Well of course I was. I just can't understand why he'd go off and join that bunch of Rebels. Isn't he supposed to be running this farm? Now who's going to do all his chores?" He was ten and just didn't care much about anything except running off whenever he could to get into more mischief.

"I guess we know who isn't," I said. His eyes, the same grey as Father's and Andrew's, flashed a look of irritation. Turning abruptly, he stomped off close behind Mother and Molly, his oversized boots clomping on the floor. Why he thought those boots were soldier like I couldn't imagine. He would have loved to have gone off to war with Andrew. He even suggested that he could be a drummer boy. Father turned a deaf ear and wouldn't even listen to him.

I stood a moment longer and watched the trail of dust as it disappeared through the mountain pass. Fergus pushed at my hand, his questioning eyes looking for a reassuring pat, his tail wagged with joy. Nanny Anna had been holding him back in the kitchen, afraid that he'd run after the retreating wagon. Now he wasn't sure what to make of the goings on.

"Fergey, I wonder if we'll ever see him again?" I shivered, not sure why I'd said that. His head tipped as if trying to understand, a quiet whine was his only response, "He's off to Frederick and then who knows where he'll be going." My hand tangled in his fur for a moment.

"Are you going to stand there all day?" He startled me. I didn't hear him come back out.

"No, Father," I answered.

"Well then, get on with whatever it is you're supposed to be doing."

"Yes, Sir," I said, and watched a moment as he made his way down the stairs. His limp slowed his progress. "Father, do you think he'll be alright?" I called after him.

"I don't know, Olivia," he said, turning back for just a moment. "I just don't know." He shook his head – in disgust maybe, I couldn't tell, then he continued on his way, down towards the barns. I watched him a moment longer, so like Andrew except for his round shoulders and the limp. If only Andrew hadn't gone. Father was dead set against it but the South needed boys and they were taking them as young as thirteen, Father said, maybe even younger.

Andrew felt he had hung back long enough; he'd been chomping at the bit to join up for two whole years. He'd argued endlessly with Father about enlisting. I think Father was just hoping it would all end before Andrew had to go. His hope had been that as the eldest son he would take over the management of the whole plantation. Andrew had other ideas however. He had never really shown much of an interest in farming, preferring books and learning. He'd once confided that he really wanted to be a lawyer like Abe Lincoln had been before he became president.

Father, however, only saw what he wanted and if he'd only paid a bit more attention, he would have known that Ryan was the farmer not Andrew. More than even being a soldier, Ryan loved roaming the fields and being down in the barns but Father usually shooed him away and told him he was too young to be part of the day-to-day management of a large farm.

All Father really wanted was to be left alone and to be able to manage and run his own place. He did not believe in the war, taking no side, anyways as far as he let on. He owned slaves but said that was only because there was no other labor available and he could not work a 1,000-acre sheep farm by himself.

It had been years ago when he had emigrated from Scotland and he felt fortunate to be a landowner. He was proud too to be an American and he could not understand why the country was fighting against itself. He was sure there had to be a better way, but hadn't yet told us what that would be.

More than once he had said that as soon as he had laborers to help he would release his slaves. Give them their freedom. By my calculations, now after all these endless months of war, the nearest able-bodied laborers, other than slaves, were probably way down in the Mexican Territory. Seemed like Andrew was the last of the boys and young men to leave. Father hung on to him as long as possible. He and Andrew rarely discussed which side was right. There had been a couple of very heated arguments and they both knew to avoid any talk of the decisions made by the south and the north.

Sometimes it seemed that Father had come just short of joining up himself. With his bad leg, chances were slim that they'd even take him no matter which side he chose. He said he was doing what he could by shipping out fresh meat for the troops and wool for their uniforms.

"Miz Olivia, what you doin' out here? You belongs in that classroom. Your Momma's goin' to be lookin' for you." Nanny bustled over looking for all the world like she was going to swat me just like she did when I was little.

"Nanny, I'm coming. I just wanted to watch Andrew."

"Well he be gone now, so you get on up to that classroom 'fore your Momma comes and takes a switch to you." Her voice was deep like it wanted to boom out but somehow she always kept it in check.

"Oh Nanny, she won't do that," I said. I breezed by her, brushing her off. It wasn't worth arguing with a slave. She had an evil look in her eye but I ignored it. I made my way up the long staircase to the classroom to "further my education" as Mother called it.

The door banged as I threw it open. They were sitting at the table waiting for me. Mother was standing ramrod straight at the front, an eyebrow raised. Her red-rimmed eyes gave the only hint that she had just bid goodbye to one of her children.

I slid into the seat next to Ryan. He was young and had all the answers to everything - he really could be an intolerable brat. Trouble was he was usually right. Molly was just eight and was still looking for all the answers. What I knew fell somewhere in between or anyways that's what Mother always said. She'd been a teacher in Atlanta, Georgia, way down in the deep south. That is up until she married Father. They'd come all the way up to the Blue Ridge area of Maryland. It was Father's fondest dream to own land and lots of it. Here he had a chance to reach that dream. It was a fine piece of land too, according to his calculation, although I didn't exactly see it that way. Most of the land was up the side of a mountain with lots of trees. Trouble was we were so far from a town or other plantation that it was nearly an all day ride just to get to talk to another living, breathing human being, anyways one that I wasn't related to.

"Olivia, I'm so glad you've decided to join us this morning." That was Mother's classroom voice. She seemed to have a different voice for every occasion. She was at the front of the room gliding from one side to the other, her long skirt swishing from side to side, an open book held in her hands. Ryan was smirking his *I'm the per-*

fect child smirk as he toyed with his pen, using it to tap out a silent drumbeat. As soon as Mother turned her back I stuck my tongue out at him. Of course I got caught.

"Olivia child, what am I going to do with you? How am I ever going to teach you to be a young lady? You truly can be a vexation." I had nothing to say. She often told me I was a vexation to her. I played with the pages of the book in front of me. "Olivia you may start this morning. Would you be kind enough to read to us about King Kenneth the First?"

Why we needed to know these things was beyond whatever I could imagine. Did anyone in the entire state of Maryland ever care about King Kenneth? I know I didn't. We spent one morning a week just studying Scottish history, Father's orders. He wanted us to be sure we were aware of our roots.

"Why did he leave?" I asked.

"King Kenneth?" asked Mother.

"No," I answered, "Why did Father leave Scotland?"

It often made the time pass a lot faster if we could get Mother to talk of something besides our studies.

"We've talked of this before you know," she

said, as she turned towards us. She brushed back a lock of escaping hair and smoothed the front of her black bombazine skirt. She used to wear light colors, like ginghams and chintz's. Now she chose only deep maroons or blacks, as if she were always in mourning or maybe she just wanted to be ready. There was an icy shiver that went down my spine.

"I know, but I forget."

Mother actually enjoyed reminiscing as much as anybody and sometimes she was interesting.

"He left because of the landowners. The workers who toiled on the big estates could never hope to own their own farms. Land was owned by the gentry only." She laid her book down on the desk and folded her hands. This was a good sign; this meant she was going to talk for awhile.

"Your father heard about America when he was quite young and never got the thought out of his head about coming to the new country to have his own farm. His father had always wanted to settle in America but he was too old to start over."

She switched without missing a beat to her teaching voice. "You know this already. Now why don't you tell us about King Kenneth of Scotland?" She had picked the book back up and that meant the discussion was closed.

The morning dragged on as Mother continued her attempt to educate and civilize us. She had often said, out of Father's hearing, that we lived in a valley of Barbarians. She didn't think much of Maryland; she was, after all, a Georgia girl. By the sounds of the tales she told us, I wished I was a Georgia girl, too. There was a real civilization down there with streets and carriages and parties and shops and lots of people my age. There were teas and cotillions and fine dresses, not at all like life on a sheep farm off somewhere on the side of a long forgotten mountain.

Mother continued to prattle on about Scottish history and by lunchtime, I was nearly asleep. I hadn't slept at all well last night.

Lunch was the usual formal affair except for the one empty seat that had so recently been vacated by Andrew. Father was at his place at the head of our table, Mother at the other end directing the meal. The table was so long they had to raise their voices just to be heard. Much of what was said seemed to echo off the wood walls and bounce off the high ceiling. The room was too large for just us. It was meant for huge parties and lots of people. There was elegance all around, but for what?

"Elbows off the table girls. Don't clatter your knife like that Ryan, it's not a weapon. Olivia, you sit up straight now, you hear. Nanny Anna, we'll be needing a bit more of those fine potatoes of yours." We could tell much of Mother's chatter aggravated Father but then he never had much to say. Except today.

"Mother," he said. "I will need to leave for awhile." My fork, loaded with sugar-cured ham was halfway to its destination when it froze in place. We three stopped what we were doing and tried to pretend we weren't listening. Father rarely left the farm, choosing to send Andrew or Elijah. This was momentous.

"And Darcy," said Mother as she laid her fork back down, "Why would you be *needing* to leave us right now?"

"You know I've been corresponding with Washington on different war matters. Well, they've decided they want me up there for a spell. It won't be long I'm sure." He popped the last of his biscuit into his mouth.

"Isn't this a bit sudden with Andrew hardly out of the county?" she asked. Her fingers smoothed an imaginary wrinkle on the table-cloth.

"Not exactly, I received word two weeks ago that I was going to have to go but I stayed on, thinking that somehow I could dissuade Andrew from enlisting." This was more than my Father had said all at one time in the entire past year. He wasn't a talker, he let Mother do that. His answers more often than not were limited to one word.

"Darcy, whatever shall we do without you? How do we care for the plantation, for Shadow Hollow?" Mother was from the south, she was loath to call our 1000-acre home a farm – to her it would always be a plantation. There was tension in her voice; she was speaking as loudly as she dared without yelling.

"Fiona, you will do perfectly well without me. You have Elijah and Big Ob to oversee the herders and the field help and Nanny Anna is perfectly capable of handling the house. I expect everything to go on as usual. I am quite sure I will not be gone that long."

"Darcy, there's a war on."

"My dear, I'm well aware of that but this must be done. You and the children will do just fine. We've yet to see any soldiers out this way. Shadow Hollow is one of the safest plantations in Maryland. They're not going to travel over these mountains and down into the valley to bother a small sheep farmer."

"But Darcy…"

He held up his hand, his knuckles knobby with age, his fingers crooked – the hands of a farmer he'd said with some pride. The discussion was over. He swabbed his napkin across his mouth, wiping off the few dribbles on the ends of a mustache that had once been a fiery red but was now splotched with gray threads. He stood, excused himself and left the room, his bad leg slowing his progress.

Mother was for once speechless. She didn't believe it was ladylike to fan one's self in public and there she was with her napkin fanning away, her usually pale face flushed to a nearly bright red.

"Oh my," she said. "Oh my, my, my." I pushed the now cold ham around my plate and made puddles with the gravy and sweet potatoes. This was usually a huge annoyance but Mother ignored it.

I stood. "Excuse me, please," I said, and left the table.

• • •

~ CHAPTER THREE ~

Early the next morning, too early, Father left. I was the only one about other than Nanny and Elijah. Often, I rose before anyone else just to have time to myself and be part of the wakening day. It could be so quiet without the two younger ones' constant chatter and I could often sneak into the library and read some of Father's books. He had an entire room of books, floor to ceiling on every wall. Many had come from Mother's home but most Father had purchased once he'd gotten to America.

When no one noticed, I would go in there and help myself to whatever I was in the mood to read that day. The good thing was that when

Nanny Anna caught me with something I probably shouldn't be reading, she couldn't read so I'd make up the title. Most times I got away with it. There was the time I was looking through a book on anatomy and Nanny snatched it from my hands and leafing through saw the pictures. I was sent to bed with no supper for the next two nights. Guess she couldn't read, but she sure knew a naked body when she saw one.

This morning with the sky still nighttime gray, I saw Father off. He had only one valise that Elijah carried to the open carriage. I stood where I had stood just yesterday, rooted to the spot on the veranda thinking maybe they should paint an outline of my feet on this very spot with my name on it so's I could always be counted on to be standing right there whenever there was a crisis.

What was happening here? There was a war going on but it was so far away we knew little about it and it had no effect on our lives other than a shortage of things like lemons and sugar. I probably wouldn't have noticed except those were the two ingredients of lemonade, my favorite drink, and we hadn't had any for the last two summers.

Father looked up at me from the carriage as he smoothed the woolen robe over his lap. His bad leg was stretched out straight in front of him. "I expect you to take care of your mother and the two young ones," he said. That was the second time in two days that someone had said that to me. I nodded, not sure how else to respond. "...and take care of Shadow Hollow," he said. I wondered what he meant as I knew little of the day to day goings on of the farm. He nodded his head. "Let's get on then Elijah," he said.

Elijah flicked the reins, saying once again his special "Ee up." He looked back once, the whites of his eyes bright in his dark face, his livery hat pulled low. Father did not look back. I stood again like yesterday and watched as they trotted down the drive. There was no trail of dust this time with the cold morning drizzle. Soon I couldn't even hear the wheels of the carriage.

Elijah would take him to where he could pick up a coach to continue his journey to Washington. Father was leaving the farm in Elijah's hands. No one else knew Shadow Hollow like Elijah, except of course Father and Andrew. It was coming up lambing season, when all the baby lambs were born. It was often the busiest time on a big farm like ours, I knew that much. It was a time when Father and Andrew rarely appeared at the dinner table, but Father said he'd be back before all that took place.

There was a cold nip in the air, like a warning. I wrapped my shawl close but it wasn't enough, I could feel the chill seeping into my bones. I looked up at my mountain. It was called Bear Mountain but it was my mountain and I had named it Mount Ursus. I had to do something with all that Latin they'd filled my head with. The peak of my mountain, often shrouded in low clouds, was barely visible against the sky as it just began to lighten. Maybe later today if no one noticed I could sneak away and go up there to walk the trails and listen to the quiet. Much as I wanted to linger on the veranda enjoying the silence, I turned and returned to the warmth of the house.

Of course, we should've known - the weather was going to change. Anyways Father and Elijah should've known and put off their trip, and I guess I should've known too. There had been a wind coming in from the north, I had felt it in the morning but thought nothing of it. By noon it was spitting snow. This wasn't a huge problem, after all we lived on the side of a mountain and were used to unexpected snowstorms even this late in the spring. But the sheep were all out there and Mother said that any number of them would be dropping their lambs in the next few weeks. It would be "prudent," as Father would say, to tend to them.

I knew so little about the goings on of our farm and had little concern about how it all worked. I didn't have to know. Father and Mother had decided long ago that they, along with Andrew and maybe someday Ryan, would deal with all matters having to do with the plantation; the two girls were to learn to be mistresses of our own future homes.

Mother spent a good deal of time teaching us the proper etiquette of serving tea, doing needlework and curtsying. Such a waste I thought. I just wanted to go away and not be part of all this. Why wouldn't they let me? I wanted to see what was on the other side of the mountain. Maybe go to Georgia or to Philadelphia – go to parties, go to the theater, talk to other people. I wanted to sprout wings and soar like an eagle and fly right over those mountains and do something, anything except spend endless days on a boring farm.

Father and Mother's intent was that we

girls would marry well; they seemed to have some vague idea of husbands for us. We really didn't have much to worry about in the husband department, it seemed about as remote a possibility of my finding a husband as my finding Abraham Lincoln rocking on our veranda. With the war on, I had not seen a man other than those related to me in well over a year. I wasn't exactly looking but it sure would've been nice to be back in the days when we enjoyed gatherings both here and at the homes of friends.

We had so much fun before the war. Mother would have parties that would last for three days. Guests would be sleeping in every room of the house. The parties were so grand that extra help had to be hired on from the outlying farms. Nanny Anna would need all the extra people she could get to take care of the cooking and all the chores. It was all just so grand. Friends would bring their children and there were girls my age to talk with and play with. We would have so much fun riding out on the horses and staying up late talking well into the night. All sorts of wonderful foods were prepared like peach shortcake and sliced honey ham and pear preserves and apple butter and icy pitchers of lemonade everywhere. We would wear party dresses of sprigged lawn with wide shiny sashes that a seamstress would be hired to specially make. Life had been so gay.

But now, not only did we not have new clothes but there was so little food. Worse yet, I was old enough now to stay up with the adults and dance until the wee hours but now there were no parties.

This day was going to drag on forever. There would be no school, as Mother said she had far too much to do. Her instructions had been that we were to study our French for the afternoon. She wouldn't notice if I didn't do it and in complete boredom I decided it was my chance to go to Father's library and pick whatever I liked to read.

Walking down the rows and rows of red and black and green and blue spines with their fine gold lettering, and trying to make up my mind, my fingers stopped on a book with the title *Gulliver's Travels*. Since that was what I would like to do most of all, travel, I decided that would be fine entertainment for the afternoon. Someday maybe there would be a book with the title *Olivia's Travels*, but I doubted it. I was going to be stuck on this horrid sheep farm until I died, I was sure of it. There was no way to escape.

I curled up in front of the hearth in Father's favorite chair, my legs tucked underneath me, which of course was when Mother bustled in the door. I pushed the book down into the cushions.

"Olivia, if you sit like that reading your eyes will cross and you'll be a hunchback. Now sit up straight and put your feet on the floor like a good girl. I need to go down to the pasture." That was her all business voice.

She bustled back out of the room with her skirts swirling behind her, not even waiting for a reply. I could hear her in the front hall pulling on her cape and then the door closing behind her. I watched out the window as she hurried through the snowflakes down towards the barns. I had no idea what she intended to do, so curled back up with my book to finish my reading.

"Miz Olivia, where your momma be?" The room had gotten dark and I rubbed my eyes to see Nanny Anna looking down at me. I guess I had fallen asleep.

"She went to the barns a while ago," I said, yawning and trying to get the sleep out of my voice. "Why?" I asked.

"She been gone a long time and Elijah 'idn't

back yet." Her voice, with its familiar deep almost guttural sound, had its usual guarded clip to it.

"Well I can't imagine where she's gone off to," I said, "I'm sure she'll be fine." I picked up my book and tried to find where I'd left off.

"Hmmm." Nanny Anna wasn't usually at a loss for things to say, but she stood there a minute and looked out into the now swirling snow. "Don't know where they're at. Miz Olivia maybe you go look for yer Momma."

"How can I do that?" I asked. "It's snowing and cold and I don't have any idea where she's gone off to."

"Well, Miz Olivia, I can go but you don't want to see me slippin' and slidin' and be spread all over that walk. You know these ol' legs don't go out in that snow." She stood in front of me, hands on hips. She had a point. If she fell, it was going to take three men to lift her back up.

"What about Ryan?" I asked but knew the answer. He was younger and could never be trusted to complete an errand in a timely manner. His wanderings had gotten him in trouble more than once.

"I'll go." I said. I let my book drop with a loud thump. She gave me that *I'm agonna swat you* look. How she could get away with being so uppity was beyond me.

Someday she was going to learn her place.

"You know how to git down to them barns?" She asked as she picked up the corner of her apron and wiped at the fingerprints on her usually shiny table. Fingerprints were not allowed in her spotless house.

"Nanny, I can certainly find my way down to the barns, I don't think I'll be needing a map." But my question was, why did I have to go? Why couldn't I stay in front of the warm fire and read my book? If mother was so foolish to go out in the storm, she should find her own way back. Sometimes I surprised myself with my laziness and lack of caring.

Nanny stood there, her chestnut colored arms crossed over her ample bosom. "You come back soon's you know somethin', hear?"

"I know, I know," The hall was dark as I pulled on my cape. Nanny Anna came up and tied the ribbon tightly around my neck. "Wear them gloves now, and you come right back, hear? Carry this lantern."

"Where's she going?" asked Ryan, as he thumped down the stairs nearly crashing into us. We never had a problem knowing where he was as there was such a clatter wherever he went.

"She goin' to find your Momma," she said. I let myself out as Ryan continued his questioning wanting to know why he couldn't go.

It took a moment to get my bearings in the swirling snow. There was just enough of the evening's gray light to make out the outlines of the barns. The snow was deep and it was icy and slippery and my feet wanted to slide right out from under me. The wind was fighting with me and it took some doing just to keep my balance. And it was cold.

I could hear Nanny close the door behind me and I could feel her eyes piercing my back. I knew she was at the window watching me.

The air sparkled with white crystals and if I weren't so cold I would have stopped to admire the flakes as they swirled and danced through the evening sky.

The wind whipped around blowing my cape in all directions; it wrapped around my legs, wanting to trip me. Shivering, I let myself disappear in the swirling white. I looked back once but the house was lost in the darkening sky and blowing snow. If Nanny held a light I couldn't see it. I was alone as the wind began to howl and the snow turned to freezing pellets that felt like icy fingers stabbing at my skin.

• • •

~ CHAPTER FOUR ~

I guess it was a good idea that Nanny made me go to fetch Mother. It took a whole lot longer than it should have; the walk was so slippery I could hardly stay standing. The wind came in icy gusts wanting to knock me over. The snow stuck to my eyelashes and stung my cheeks. Nanny Anna really should have been the one to have gone but she hated the snow and almost never went further than the front veranda when there was ice on the ground or if snow was even threatening.

Why Father and Mother put up with her insolence and peculiarities I just couldn't imagine. Nanny had said that once in Atlanta she'd slipped on some ice and had hurt her knee so badly that she still felt it. Mother told me it wasn't the injured knee so much as it was the fact that they couldn't get her up. It had been so slippery and she was so big it had taken three other slaves to right her and that was after she'd spent hours on the freezing ground. Nanny'd never forgotten it, and it certainly was an inconvenience when she should have been the one to go out in the freezing cold.

Sometimes I wondered just what went on in my head. I'm so cussed lazy sometimes I thought. So often I just didn't want to do anything, especially go out into a roaring snowstorm while our slave sat by the warm fire.

The wind had picked up some since morning and was blowing through the trees making a clatter in the leafless branches. Holding the lantern up, I tried to find my way. It was like being inside a great big feather pillow. Puffy white flakes so thick it was hard to see. A gust of wind plowed down the side of the mountain and pouf, it snuffed out the flame in my lantern. Fine, I thought, now I've got to wander around in the dark by myself.

"Fergus," I called, my voice shaky and unnatural. I hardly expected to see his long tail wagging but there was always hope. What if there were soldiers hiding behind the trees? A shiver snuck down my back. It occurred to me that we were out here all alone. Andrew was gone. Father was gone and who knew where Elijah was. The realization of how really desolate and lonely this farm was sent another shiver snaking down my spine.

I guess I never realized that none of the responsibility of the farm had ever been left to us. I didn't like it – why weren't the others here doing what they were supposed to be doing. Why was this suddenly falling on my shoulders? I knew nothing of the day-to-day operation of running a plantation and besides, I was cold, my fingers had turned to ice, and though I was loath to admit it, I was scared nearly out of my wits.

It was hard to listen to everything at once, a snapped twig, the plop of snow falling from some branch; it was impossible to distinguish anything with the noise of the wind. All sorts of awful images popped into my imagination. Yesterday's bad dream started to prick at the edges of my mind. "Go way bad dream, go way," I muttered again and again trying to shake it out of my head. My whispers were big puffs of white in the frozen night. Pay attention, I thought, concentrate on where you're headed.

"Fergus," I called again, trying to make my voice more confident. Why wasn't he here? I squinted into the darkness. The barns could still be seen between bursts of snowflakes, the gray outlines just barely visible. I started to hum, trying to listen to my own voice, trying to drown out the wailing of the wind and the clattering of the dead branches and the thoughts that kept wanting to torment me.

My favorite tune played around in my head, a lullaby that Nanny Anna always sang to us when we were little and would wake in the night. She'd rock us back and forth and hold us against her warmth and the comfort of all the kitchen smells that clung to her. Her deep baritone voice always managed to soothe us as we settled back down.

The daylight be fading
My soul it be quieting
There be peace all around
As my burdens be laid down"

I couldn't remember all the words but let the few lines I did remember dance about in the wind.

The barns were no longer there as they had disappeared in the swirl of snow, and I just hoped that my frozen feet were headed in the right direction.

It did come to mind that we weren't really allowed down this way, so I didn't know much about the barns and the fields and all the goings on with the animals. We were always kept close to the house except of course when we went on carriage rides to visit, which was rare. The territory down by the barns was usually discouraged. When we went for rides, or "airings," as Mother called them, Big Ob or one of the others would bring up the horses. They would be saddled and ready or they would bring the carriage round if we were heading off for an afternoon of "visiting." We didn't get to ride very often. I looked forward to the time when I could someday gallop off by myself and not always be chaperoned so closely. It was exciting to ride into the mountains but it was always with Father or Andrew and it didn't happen very often. Of course, we young ones were never alone. Not Ryan of course, he'd sneak off at any opportunity.

It wasn't fair. More than anything I wanted to ride like the boys and not have to be bothered with balancing on a sidesaddle keeping my skirts properly tucked about me. How could one ride off sitting on that awkward contraption? Someday I was going to do it, I was sure of it. I was going to ride like the wind and just keep going 'til maybe I fell off the edge of the earth.

Father's plan had been that he would deal with all the farm matters and he would teach Andrew everything there was to know about the wool business and raising sheep. He said Molly and I were to learn to deal with the household things. This was tiresome to say the least and it seemed some days my only escape was to go walking into the mountains. As long as I didn't say too much about where I'd go, no one seemed to mind, which suited me just fine. Father had different fenced areas all up and down the side of the mountain so I could always find my way.

Lost in my own thoughts I jumped when a cold nose poked at me. An icy shiver raced up my spine; I nearly slid to the ground as Fergus gave a yip of welcome. I wanted to hug him, I was so glad to see that lump of shaggy fur. It was so cold and I was so alone in the swirl of icy flakes. He nudged my arm again to let me know he was there. Snow was piling up on the black fur of his back but he didn't care.

We had three sheep dogs; two were almost always with the sheep. Fergus was my favorite. He wasn't very good at herding so could often be found in the gardens or around the barns. Mother would never have let him in the house but Nanny had him the kitchen now and again when no one was paying too close attention. He was a wonderful dog, all dark and shaggy except for the white patch on his chest.

"I'm so glad you're here," I said. My fingers tangled in the warmth of his fur, as I brushed off the snow. "Where's Mother?" I asked as though he were going to answer. "Glad I found you old friend."

It felt much better walking along with someone even though that someone was just Fergus. "Come along, we'll go find her." He wagged his tail sending snowflakes scattering. Trying not to slip, I worked to get my feet to move faster, holding my cloak tight against the wind. The snow was prickling my cheeks and sticking to my eyelashes and the dampness was seeping into the seams of my boots. My toes were getting numb.

"We'll start here," I said pushing open the door. It creaked in protest. It was one of three barns and I had no idea, which Mother would have gone to, or even if she'd seek shelter in one of the barns. The warmth was wonderful. The sheep and few cows that stayed in the huge wooden structure kept it almost balmy even on the coldest days. I stepped inside, frozen through to the bone, wondering what was next if she couldn't be found.

• • •

~ CHAPTER FIVE ~

A warm glow of light spilled from the corner. "Mother," I yelled and watched as the sheep shifted nervously. Yelling was not a good thing around sheep, I knew that much. If one got spooked and decided to run, the entire herd would more than likely follow. I said it again but not so loud. "Is it you," I whispered into the darkness.

"Over here," she said, "Please don't shout." This was a new voice, one that sounded almost feeble, not one that I'd heard before. She was tucked up on an old wooden bench with one of the horse blankets pulled around her. One of her high-topped boots was lying on its side in the straw.

"What's happened?" I asked.

Mother rarely sat down, she moved the entire day seeing to this and seeing to that and always straightening something. She was never still.

"My ankle, unfortunately," she said. "I was outside holding open the gate for the sheep and the wind caught it. It slammed against my ankle, I'm sorry to say." She pulled back the blanket, the black and blue swelling was nearly as big as an orange. "It may be broken, but I don't think so. Probably just bruised." By the look of it, and I knew little about body parts, I'd have said broken for sure.

"We need to get you to the house," I said. "Where's Elijah and where are the herders?"

"Elijah has not returned. I suspect the roads are probably terrible." She winced as she tried to readjust her leg. "Big Ob was here when I came down but I'd asked him to bring the rest of the sheep down off the mountain. He's up there with the others probably trying to herd them all.

"Why not just leave them?" I asked. I knew little of the goings on of sheep and cared even less, to me they were nothing more than a dumb animal that kept us in lamb stew and warm woolen shawls all winter.

"Well, you know dear, that some will be lambing soon and need to be cared for and we don't know how long this storm will last. We've got to get those ewes back in the barns." Mother's fingers picked at the blanket pulling off tiny bits of straw.

"Fine," I said, "and how should we get you back to the house? You can't stay here."

"Perhaps I will. I can wait until Elijah or the herders return and they can bring me up."

"Mother, they may not return until the middle of the night, if then. We need to get you home before you get too chilled and by the looks of it someone needs to see to that ankle."

"Olivia child, I can't walk. I'll be fine here. You go on back up to the house and I'll wait."

Well, walking back up that hill alone in a blinding snowstorm was not what I wanted to do, but trying to bring Mother back with me may be even worse. She could not stay down in the barn alone waiting for who knows how long until one of the slaves returned. It could be all night and I certainly was not going to spend the night with her in a drafty old barn. The herders may well be caught up in the storm and who knew when they'd get back down.

Her normally pale cheeks were nearly rosy red with the cold and I could see her tremble or shiver every now and again. "Mother, remember that sled that they used to bring up firewood? Do we still have it?"

"I'm sure it's tucked away somewhere, probably hanging on a wall in one of our out buildings," she said, "Perhaps in one of the barns." She stopped for a moment, "I know exactly where it is," she said. "Look in the next barn; it should be back in the far corner."

Fergus came with me as I slipped and slid between the barns. The snow was not letting up. The flakes were like thick icy goose down blowing through the air making it hard to see.

The sled was in the next barn, right where Mother said it would be. Of course, I thought. She's never wrong.

The snow was deep enough so that the wooden runners glided nicely in the iciness. Bringing it almost inside the barn, I helped Mother hobble over to it and then settled her in a sitting position, her legs hung off the back wrapped in the horse blanket. Settling her was easy enough, getting her back to the house was going to be another matter entirely.

My trail of footsteps coming from the house had long ago been filled by the whiteness, leaving no trace at all that I'd ever even been there. Mother held her lantern trying to light the path and gave instructions as to the easiest way back in the blowing snow.

"Why did Father have to build his house on a hill," I asked, the wind ripping the words from my mouth. I'd hardly noticed it before but now it seemed like it was set practically on top of a mountain.

I didn't think Mother had heard me with the blowing wind. She had, and then had to raise her voice to answer. "He built Shadow Hollow because it reminded him so much of the manor houses of Scotland."

"The ones he couldn't go in?" I asked, watching the wind snatch my words away.

She ignored me. "Olivia dear, why don't you leave me here and go get some help to pull the sled."

"Who would that be Mother?" Icy white puffs came out of my mouth with every word. She sighed, I was the sassy daughter, the one that was a constant vexation to her, the one who always had something to say, most often when I should have held my tongue.

"I'm sorry Olivia that you had to come out in this." There was a tremor in her voice. She must be freezing I thought.

"Well there was no one else to do it Mother, so I don't mind." The rope pulling the sled had sliced through my gloves and was cutting into my fingers. That was all right 'cause I could hardly feel it; my fingers were numb from the cold. The rise to the house was much steeper than I remembered it. As small as Mother was, she certainly was a load to pull.

"Stop for awhile child and catch your breath. I'm warm enough and there's certainly no rush." Her words were barely audible between gusts of wind.

"I'm fine." My heart felt like it had jumped up into my throat it was beating so hard. My nose was dripping faster than I could tend to it and my feet were now soaked and half frozen. I wasn't sure if I could still feel my toes.

"Why did you come out in this?" I asked, trying not to sound quite so peevish and exhausted. I decided I had to stop for a moment to catch my breath.

"And who else would there be? Someone needed to check on the herders with Elijah gone; they don't always take the initiative you know."

"Why doesn't Father get more help?" I asked, squinting into the distance trying to see the house.

"Who and where would he get the help? There is no one else. We're really not supposed to have slaves anymore and the entire county is off fighting the War. There is no one left."

I knew about the part that every able-bodied man was off fighting the war, but that slavery was no longer allowed was going to have to be for another day. Father didn't believe in owning living, breathing human beings but why then did we have Elijah and Nanny Anna and the others? At least she didn't say, "There's a war on you know" like everyone else felt they needed to tell me.

"When will it ever be over?" I asked. I had started pulling the sled again and it was actually going faster if she kept talking.

"No one knows," she said. "It's not looking particularly good right now for the South, so perhaps it will end soon and then Father and Andrew will return home." She was trying to help by pushing the sled along with her hands.

"Where did Father go?" I stopped again to catch my breath. The snow danced and swirled around us and for a moment I wondered what would happen if we lost our way.

"We're not sure where he's gone off to. He said he was needed in Washington, but I'm not so sure. It's not my place to ask." Her breath was in little puffy gasps. "He has his business to tend to. He manages quite well selling his wool. He'll be fine. We shouldn't worry. I know the sheep and I know the routine."

"Why would you want to be tending to sheep when we have Elijah and Big Ob?" My breath was coming in short gasps, each word a new puff of white in the freezing air.

"There are times like this when I'm needed," she answered. "Long ago when you were very little, and the herd was much smaller, I did most of the tending. But then there were so few sheep it wasn't terribly difficult and your father needed the help."

I was listening but my thoughts were wandering and what came to mind was that I need to rename my mountain. Note to self: call it Mount Magnus as in huge; it was feeling a lot higher and mightier than Mount Ursus, which I'd named it earlier.

I wasn't sure if I'd be able to drag the sled the rest of the way. Mother was trying to make the time pass with a stream of chatter. Some words disappeared into the wind, but I could hear most of what she said.

"I can remember carding the wool, and spinning the wool and even weaving. You wouldn't remember that, you were too small." She stopped a moment and let her thoughts drift. "Nanny Anna and I spent many an afternoon together throwing the shuttle back and forth while we wove yards and yards of woolen fabric. Now we send it all off to be done, so I just step in when needed."

The snow was falling in over the tops of my boots but the sled glided smoothly. "Tell me again," I said, "Why do they call this Bear Mountain?" which was actually the real name, much as I wanted it renamed to Mount Ursus or Mount Magnus. Maybe this wasn't the best tale to tell in the dark but I wanted to make the time pass. I was exhausted.

"Well, I know you've heard all of this before, but the tale is that there was a mountain man who cut through the hollow to get his furs to market that he'd trapped in Ken'tuck. On one of his trips, he'd heard screams and cries coming out of the forest. He wasn't at all sure of what it was so he went to investigate. It sounded like a baby."

We stopped under one of our huge spreading oaks. My feet were threatening to stop moving and my hands may as well have been two blocks of frozen ice. I could hear Mother shifting, trying to get comfortable. "Let's stop for just a minute," she said, sounding almost as breathless as me.

"Fine," I croaked, my voice raspy from the icy cold. "Tell me the rest of the story." I tucked my hands up under my arms trying to find some warmth.

She was not anxious to go on but sitting like two frozen statues wasn't going to work. She started again but with little enthusiasm. "He snuck up on the cries, which by now had become whimpers and there it was. A bear cub with its paw caught in one of those traps, like the kind that they use for beaver. That little thing didn't know what to do but kept shaking its paw. It was biting at the trap, but of course it wasn't coming off." The wind had shifted and for just a moment calmed, letting the snowflakes dance in the quiet.

Mother had her second wind. "As everyone knows," she continued, "One never gets near a cub as its mother is probably lurking about somewhere in the bushes."

She didn't have to add that a mother bear is about the most dangerous thing that's ever walked the earth should anyone dare to interfere with her cub.

"Well that mountain man took some time watching that cub to be sure it's momma wasn't hiding in a tree or just out foraging somewhere and just waiting to spring on whoever got near her baby. When he was sure that that little cub was on its own, he approached it as carefully as possible, knowing the sharpness of its claws. He threw his blanket over her so's he could pry open the trap without getting clawed."

Again she paused, she was getting tired and cold. I was sorry there wasn't something warm to drink to revive her, but she continued. "It took some time with the cub squirming so, but he did get that trap open. He let that baby untangle itself from the blanket sure she was going to come after him. Well that cub was so dazed and in such pain, she sat there for a bit and eyed that mountain man. After a bit she just up and ran away, favoring that mangled paw."

I knew the rest of the story so didn't have to hear every word, so only half listened as I took up the rope to drag the sled the rest of the way.

It's said that after a few years when that mountain man was heading through that same hollow, a bear took off after him – he thought he was a goner for sure. The tale goes that out of nowhere another bear appeared and about took that old grizzly apart that was chasing him.

Mother sneezed and I lost some of her words but she continued: "He noticed that the black bear was using only three paws, the fourth one hung at an odd angle. The mountain man was saved and so the story goes that forever more no one traveling over this mountain has ever been bothered again by a bear."

I loved the story. True or not it gave the mountain a nice feeling. "There's the house," I said. Just in time I thought, my feet had no feeling. I don't think I could've gone another step. Nanny Anna was in the window holding a candle. In fact there were candles lit in every window of the house.

"My, doesn't she just think of everything," said Mother. "She's guiding us home; she knows how dark it is out here." Yes, I thought, but why isn't she out pulling this sled instead of me!

It took Ryan and Molly and me to get Mother up the veranda stairs and into the house. Nanny Anna took over from there bustling about and giving orders to everyone. In minutes, she had Mother wrapped in a warm blanket on the davenport, in front of a blazing fire. The warmth filled the room and shadows danced across the walls. She looked chilled through. Her lips were nearly white against the red of her cheeks and every now and again a shiver shook her whole body.

"Miz Olivia, now you go on up and you get out of them clothes. There be a fire laid for you in your room, you go on up there and I be bringin' soup up by and by." She waved her hands at me to get me to scoot. I did.

It felt wonderful to crawl into my bed in my long nightgown, the flannel soft and warm. Nanny Anna had even thought to put a warmed brick down by my feet. Not sure if that soup ever made it to my room 'cause I think I was asleep before I'd even snuggled down into my feather pillow.

~

The purple and white crocuses had already flowered, the tulips were just beginning to unfold from their tight buds, and Mother was still sick. After our late spring storm, an infection had settled in her lungs. Nanny said it was probably a good thing because it kept her still so's her ankle could heal. When Nanny couldn't keep her down any longer, she would take short walks around the house leaning heavily on her cane.

Elijah dealt with the herders and Mother directed from the drawing room, seated at her huge mahogany desk. Nanny kept a footrest close by so's she could prop her leg while she worked. School had been sketchy. There was too much to do directing the entire house and farm to worry about our education. It was a wonderful break for us and I tried hard to stay away so's no one would notice that we weren't spending time in the classroom.

It had been six weeks and still there was no word from Father. Mother tried to pretend that she wasn't worried but there were new lines around her eyes and she fidgeted endlessly now that she couldn't do her incessant puttering about the house. Her knitting was always close by and whenever she wasn't working on the farm ledgers or giving orders, she would pick up her needles, the clicking echoing throughout the house. It was eerie, as often it was the only sound heard. It seeped into every room and eve-

ry corner - the non-stop sound of those wooden
needles.

Her constant knitting did of course benefit
all of us. Everyone in the family, including
Nanny Anna, had long triangular shawls. Molly's and Nanny's were dyed an indigo blue color.
Mine was more of a rectangular shape. It was
thick and soft and buff colored, the natural color
of the sheep's wool. Mother said it went well
with the darkness of my eyes. Ryan had two
very warm sweaters that he alternated through
the winter, wearing the grey one day and the
blue the next. They'd gotten a bit shabby but
kept him toasty warm through the cold months.

When Mother's needles weren't clicking, her
cane was tap, tapping. Since she'd been laid up
with her ankle, she'd been using a cane to aid
her walking. She'd go from room to room and
out to the veranda but didn't go much further.
Between the click of her knitting needles and
the thump, thumping of her cane, we always
knew where she was.

With all her busy-ness it was hard to tell if
her lung infection was getting better or worse.
There was a new cough that I hadn't heard before and often it would rattle through the house
during the night hours.

Now I wonder why we didn't keep her confined to her big four poster in her bedroom. Why
did we let her get up and force herself to walk?
She probably wouldn't have died if she'd been in
bed when the Yankees came.

. . .

~ CHAPTER SIX ~

A cold drizzle was blowing through the air.
April showers bring May flowers or so we'd been
told. And there were a few, like the scattered
brave violets that were poking their purple
heads through the leftover snow. With the late
chill it was unlikely that we'd see many more of
the early spring blooms. Even the apple blossoms were still tight little brown buds looking
as though they'd had second thoughts about
spreading their cheery pink petals this year.

Mother heard the riders first. I'm sure she
thought it must be Father finally returning
home. We had been sitting in the front parlor
learning all the details of cross-stitching. Moth-

er had once again been trying to correct the piece of puckered fabric that I couldn't seem to flatten and keep straight, no matter how much effort I put into it. My colors seemed fine enough but that's all that was fine. My piece had soiled edges and it was near impossible to get the stitches to be even. There were bumps and snags and far too many knots. It was so exasperating. Mother would look at it and click her tongue the way she did to show how I was such a vexation to her. It was often such a mess that she'd even given up snipping the threads so's I could do it over. At some point she must have realized that there are a few of us who just aren't made for the finer things in life.

She had just finished shaking her head over my tight, too large stitches, when she hobbled over to one of the long front windows. Glad for the distraction, I'm sure, she stared out the window. There was excitement in her eyes but then she gasped; her hand went up to her throat. Her voice wavered, "Quick, children, you must hide. Run now, fast. It's the Yankees. Good Heavens, they've found us."

We didn't want to run. We wanted to stay and see a real Yankee soldier. This the most excitement we'd ever had. We didn't want to miss it. We wanted to see if they really did have horns and blew fire out of their nostrils like we'd been told.

"You heard me, remove yourselves immediately." She came very close to raising her voice but thumped her cane instead. "Go. Don't come back down until I send for you."

Nanny Anna appeared as if she'd been just outside the door waiting for her instructions. She had that look in her eye. It was the look that those monstrous brown eyes of hers said none of us was too big for her to go find a switch if we didn't mind. Ryan and Molly stood rooted to the spot. Molly was speechless, eyes wide, filled with fear, too large in her freckled face. Ryan gave me that: You can't scare me look. They were not going to move.

"Come on. We've got to go." Grabbing Molly's hand and using the other to push Ryan through the door, we headed for the stairs.

"Hurry," said Mother. "I'll speak with them and see what I can do."

We ran up two flights of stairs and climbed the ladder up into the ceiling. I pushed open the trap door and we scrambled into the attic. Father had worked out the plan long ago. If soldiers ever came, we were to hide and hide fast he had said. Young girls should never be seen by soldiers and he feared for Ryan, that he'd be snatched up and pressed into service even though he was far too young.

We let the trapdoor slam shut behind us, it sounded like the crack of a bullet. The space was dark and dusty with cobwebs hanging from the rafters in thin wispy tendrils. An old loom pushed into one corner poked through the shadows; thick dust covered the strings. A few dusty chairs with either a broken leg or broken back were tucked here and there and two old trunks were pushed against the eaves where we could sit. It wasn't exactly inviting. I snuck over to the end window. The dust was so thick it was nearly impossible to see out but bits of the conversation drifted up.

"What are they doing," whispered Ryan.

"Shush," I hissed. "I need to listen. They're laughing. I can't understand what they're saying, they're too far away."

My curiosity got the better of me. I needed to see for myself. I turned and tiptoed back to the trapdoor.

"Olivia, what are you doing?" asked Ryan.

"Nothing, stay here," I hissed at him.

In silence I crept down the ladder then

down the stairs and slipped into the kitchen. Mother was still standing at the window and if she heard me she didn't turn. The kitchen door was ajar and I stepped outside watching through the drizzly rain as they rode up the drive. They were laughing, jostling each other and in no great hurry to get out of the rain. A bottle was passed between them and I watched as they each swiped at their mouths with their sleeves already grimy with who knows what.

They left the drive and trotted up through the apple trees, reining in their horses. I froze. Too late I thought. My legs wouldn't move. A fear crept up my back and I shivered. This was the dream I'd had.

The three dismounted and walked towards me, their rifles slung casually under their arms. They looked so like my dream although they weren't breathing flames and their eyes weren't the fiery red that I remembered.

My feet wouldn't move. I gasped in horror as the laughing faces turned into sneers and came towards me. Their uniforms were disheveled, if they could even be called uniforms. They were close to rags with buttons missing and tears and seams worn through. The one closest said something very crude but I hardly even heard. My ears were filled with a rushing sound of terror. I needed to get away. The tallest one reached out to grab at me when I heard Mother's voice.

"Sir," she called out, "May I help you?" They turned in the direction of the voice as my feet remembered how to work. Silently I whirled around and was back in the kitchen before they even knew I was gone.

Mother was asking if they wanted food. I couldn't hear it all. Nanny Anna was out there too. I could hear her voice but not what she was saying. There was much back and forth discussion. I tried to creep back up the stairs. The sound of the gravely voices and the occasional deep laugh from one of the soldiers traveled easily through the open door.

I had just reached the attic ladder when Mother's voice suddenly rose to a scream and Nanny, her voice booming out in a threatening tone I'd never heard, yelled, "You get yer dirty Yankee hands off'n her."

It sounded like a struggle. I didn't need to see what was happening. They weren't going to get away with that. Shots were fired. Ryan threw open the trapdoor and slid down the ladder, landing with a loud thump at the bottom.

"I'm going out there," he said, with a bravado that I'm sure he didn't feel.

It must have taken seconds only to get back down the stairs. The front door was letting in the blowing rain. Out on the lawn, plain as anything, there were two bodies. They were lying in awkward positions in the mud. Blood was seeping from holes in their uniform jackets. There was a third one. He was tearing down the drive, his horse pounding and splashing through the mud in a wild stampede. The rider was whipping his horse for all he was worth. Mother had dropped her cane. Nanny Anna had her arm around her trying to steer her towards the house. Elijah stood just to one side of the house, a rifle in his hand, hot smoke rising from the barrel. There was blood seeping from a wound in his shoulder.

"Mother," I screeched and ran to her side. It was hard to stop hugging her. She was drenched from the rain. Nanny was on one side and I was on the other, as we half carried and half walked her back into the house. "She be fine, she be fine," Nanny said over and over.

What to do? Everything was in chaos. Nanny was helping Mother walk, Molly was crying; near hysterics. It took a harsh command from Nanny to silence her. I ran to the kitchen for water. Mother and Nanny shuffled along behind me. Elijah was sitting on the floor in the kitchen. Blood was everywhere.

"Tend to his wound first, Nanny. I'll be fine," said Mother.

"Mother, get back to the front room and lie on the divan. We'll get help. Ryan get the fire going." I was giving commands left and right, trying to get them out of the kitchen.

"I don't have to take orders from you," Ryan mumbled under his breath but then looked over at Mother and decided he would.

"What should we do?" I asked, as we settled her on the divan. "There are two bodies out there. Mother, what happened?"

"They'd been drinking," she said. "They wouldn't leave." She laid back, her face ghost like.

"But one got away," I said. "Won't he be back?"

"He could," she said, "But by the looks of how shabby they were, I suspect they weren't in the Army but had deserted."

"We need to get rid of them." Ryan looked at me. "The bodies," I said, "We need to be rid of them."

Get rid of them? Two grown men? I went

back outside to take another look. The rain splattered my dress; a shiver ran down my spine. I'd never seen a dead person before and how were we supposed to know if they were really dead? The rain had washed away most of the blood on the first one. He had a scraggly beard, now soaked by the drizzle. There was a patch where one eye should have been. His other eye stared straight up as if looking for something that no one else could see. It gave me the willies but I could see there was no breath left in him. I took my handkerchief and placed it over his face, trying not to touch him. The rain quickly plastered it to him like a mask.

The other had fallen flat and thankfully I couldn't see his face. There was no breath left in either of them that was for sure. Not only were they no longer alive but good heavens they were big. What would we do with them? How soon would the other one be back? Bury them, I thought. Bury them before the herders come down off the mountain to see what's been done and before anyone else should come by. I didn't know what else we could do with them.

The ground was slippery with the rain but I ran down to the barn and searched for shovels. Nanny Anna, whether she wanted to or not, was going to have two Yankee deserters buried in her kitchen garden. The chickens squawked and flew off in all different directions as I ran back up the hill dragging the two shovels. Grabbing Ryan and giving orders to Molly to stay with Mother, I pulled him out the door.

"This is what we're going to do," I said. "We're going to bury them and we're going to bury them now. So pick up that shovel and start digging."

Ryan was very nearly speechless, but not quite. "Does it have to be so close to the house," he asked, his voice wavering for a moment.

"And where else? We can't drag them far, they're too big. The ground here is soft and it shouldn't be too hard to shovel. Hurry," I said.

Nanny Anna came out to check the progress.

"What of Elijah?" I asked.

"It be his shoulder. He won't be doin' much for a spell."

"What happened?" I asked between throwing shovels full of dirt.

"They want to take your Momma inside and want to know where you was. She try to talk 'em out of it. They was just plain bein' ugly. Your Momma wouldn't let 'em anywheres near you."

"What'd they want with Olivia?" asked Ryan.

"Shut up, Ryan," I said. Why would he even ask that?

"They seen Elijah come 'round the corner wif that gun. The tall one wif that red hair, he fire at Elijah, he'd a kilt him if he'd taken better aim."

"I thought slaves couldn't have guns." My back was hurting from the digging and there were blisters already on my hands that were popping open and making my hands sting.

"That be true," she said but added nothing more.

"Well, here Nanny you should be doing this." She took the shovel while I went down for one more look. They had come on horses but both had run off and I wasn't about to try to find them. A large gun was lying in the mud and for whatever reason I grabbed it and ran up to the house with it. In the kitchen Elijah was resting, stretched out on the hearth, his shoulder bandaged. His face was a dusky gray and he looked like he was sleeping.

"Miz Olivia," he said, opening one eye. "Didn't mean to hurt those two, they was gonna kill your Momma."

"Elijah, where'd you get the gun?" I asked.

"Why your pap taught me to shoot long ago. How'm I gonna protect those sheep from wolves and mountain lions without a gun," he said as he cradled the wounded arm. "I'm no David you know, but can often hit what I aims at" he sighed. Elijah knew his Bible stories.

"Elijah, I had no idea."

"Think it's time someone taught you," he said. "Think maybe it'd be what yer pap would want about now." He nodded at the gun I was still holding. "Guess that one's gonna be about as good as any to learn on."

"Elijah, that Yankee that got away will probably be back. If that happens I don't know what we're going to do. Heaven knows what they'll be up to next."

"Yep," he said. "And then again maybe not. Them three look like ruffians to me. More'n likely they be deserters."

I laid the gun on Nanny's scrubbed smooth kitchen table. "Better hide that," he said. "I teach you to shoot, then I stay outa the way for a spell. T'aint no one knows how to shoot here better than me, and this be my shootin' arm." He patted his bandaged shoulder, wincing when his fingers touched the wound.

~

We got them buried all right. It took three of us to drag them to the holes we'd prepared for them. Nanny, no matter about her bad knees, had to help. They were just too big for Ryan and me and I didn't want Molly out there. The holes we dug weren't any too deep but then they were Yankee deserters and I wasn't about to do anything special for the likes of them. I'd never seen a lifeless body before and wasn't happy to see one now. It took us most of the afternoon but when we finished, there wasn't a trace. Nanny Anna said to just put it out of our minds as best we could.

Not so easy, putting bad things out of your head. It wasn't too many days later when she asked why I was being so wasteful with the candles. I didn't tell her that my room felt a whole lot better with the light from a candle so's I could fall asleep without seeing visions of dead soldiers in every corner.

~

It seemed like it wasn't more than two weeks after we'd dug the holes when little shoots of green started poking through the soil where Nanny had put in her spring onions. She said it was going to be the best garden ever this year. I certainly hoped so 'cause our dinners had become awfully meager. Mother said nothing about our lack of food, but we were going without at most meals. Sometimes no bread, other times just water, no cider and none of the watered down wine, and even though we did have lamb to eat, it was becoming far too often. Most nights we would go to bed hungry and then get up hungry. How were we ever to get through this?

. . .

~ CHAPTER SEVEN ~

Mother died. It was the time when the blue-bells put on their spring show, running along the stream and half way up the mountain. She loved the Virginia bluebells. She'd often said she was sorry they didn't last the whole year. They were close to the color of Molly's eyes, maybe that's why she loved them so much, the blue-bells I mean. My eyes were much darker, sort of like Father's, but I don't think anyone had ever really noticed.

Nanny Anna had been with Mother night and day since those soldiers had come. She slept on the floor next to her bed. She wouldn't leave except to prepare a meal. Between Elijah with his bad shoulder and Nanny with her bad knees, they had managed to get Mother up the stairs to her own bed. There had been a roaring fire most of the day and night. The room felt overly hot, with the cloying smell of camphor clinging to every scrap of clothing or piece of bedding. The lung infection had never really gone away from when she'd hurt her ankle in the blizzard. Then getting soaked to the bone when those soldiers came made it worse than ever.

Each night I would slip into her room to give her a good night kiss; it was frightening to see how pale she'd gotten and how dry and hot she felt. It looked as though her skin had been stretched tight over her cheekbones. There were new deep blue circles around her eyes.

Nanny had made a mustard plaster that she laid on her chest and she tucked warm bricks next to her feet. She looked so small and frail. I tried to talk with her but she would only nod now and again, but then one afternoon, while Nanny took her leave for a few minutes, she spoke. Her voice was barely above a whisper.

"Olivia child, take care. You're all they have." She hadn't even opened her eyes but she knew it was me. She took a raspy breath. "You must remember child that life isn't always fair. I'm sorry for that." Her eyes fluttered her fingers picked at the coverlet, her voice was nearly a whisper. "There will be times of great challenge but you, of all my children, have the strongest will and a determination and a strength that will see you through." Her breath was in short gasps. "Please," she continued, "Don't ever give up." The words trailed off and then she abruptly fell into a deep sleep, her chest rising and falling with her shallow breathing.

Nanny tried to tell us before it happened that she'd seen sickness like this before and few of them made it through. But I thought what does she know and wouldn't listen. But it happened anyway.

This time the herders dug the grave. Elijah brought them down from the mountain and had them dig the hole. We could hear it from the house. I tried to cover my ears but it didn't work. The sound of the shovels digging through the rocky ledge must have echoed through the whole valley.

Our little procession followed the wood box up the hill. The coffin was so newly made it smelled of pine and was still weeping sap. The hole they dug was between Sarah Jane, who would have been my older sister, had she lived longer than her two years. Stuart John, was on the other side. A little brother, who never took his first breath.

The fence protecting the little graveyard leaned on one side. Father had talked of fixing it but hadn't yet gotten to it. The two little gravestones had moss creeping up the sides, looking much older than they really were. Mother had made it part of her weekly schedule to walk up to the gravesites and weed and clear and trim the grass, and talk to her two departed children. There was even a bench set next to the fence so's she could sit if she wanted. She didn't. She had said it made her happy just to be around them, the two she'd lost. Maybe she wondered why they had not lived and some of her others had? Odd that she'd kept that attachment to two that had died so long ago.

We three stood in a line as we looked down into a dark hole. It was so hard to imagine what we were doing. That was my mother in the pine box. How had this happened? Where was Father? Why wasn't Andrew here? I don't know why I couldn't understand what was happening but I couldn't seem to accept or realize that she would no longer be with us. I wanted to pinch myself to wake up from this bad dream. I was sure I'd walk back into the house and she'd be there bustling around to get everything done. I could see her so clearly, how could she now be in that coffin that they'd lowered into that dark hole that didn't seem to have a bottom?

Nanny Anna made us leave. We stood like three statues not knowing what to do and it was raining again. Raining on the bluebells that covered the side of the mountain; raining into that dark hole that had no bottom. The herders were standing, leaning on their shovels waiting for the nod from Elijah to start filling in that yawning black pit. Nanny all but pushed us out of the fenced area to get us to move. There was work to do and they needed to get on with their business. The rain was beating down; the umbrella that she held couldn't protect all of us.

We were halfway to the house when I heard the first shovelful of dirt hit the pine box. A shiver shook me to my bones. It felt like icy fingers were poking me all over. As I turned Nanny put herself between me and what went on in the graveyard.

"Keep goin' Miz Olivia, we's almost home." Her brown hand, work worn from too many years of tending to too many things, took my arm as if guiding me. "You got a farm to run child."

• • •

~ CHAPTER EIGHT ~

Where to start? How could I run a sheep farm? I knew nothing of sheep. We'd hardly been allowed in the barns and almost never around the animals and here we were with nearly 1,000 acres, 400 sheep or more, chickens, a couple of cows and horses that hadn't been tended to in so long they'd probably forgotten what a saddle felt like.

We owned four slaves who were herders, a foreman and an uppity house slave. We had no money that I knew of and I had no idea what needed to be done, and furthermore, I didn't want any part of it. I wanted a new dress, I wanted new shoes, I wanted to ride out in the carriage, I wanted to have some friends, I wanted my Mother, oh how I wanted my Mother. But I wanted a life; I wanted something besides everyone looking at me thinking I had answers. Most of all though, I just wanted to sleep. I pulled the quilt up closer and burrowed down into the feather pillow. It was warm and comfortable and dark and safe as long as I kept my eyes closed.

"Miz Olivia you get yo'self up this minute." I'd know that voice anywhere. The voice that wanted to boom through the hallways but somehow kept itself restrained was now standing over me. I burrowed deeper into the pillow. What gave her the right to be bothering me so early in the morning?

"Get outa that bed now," she said. "You don't wanna make me angry this mornin'." She was tapping her foot as she spoke.

Letting a loud groan escape, I rolled over and there she was, her arms folded, her turban wrapped head shaking back and forth, her huge brown eyes boring into me. They were eyes that were hard and soft all at the same time. Eyes that saw everything and told nothing. "Get outa dat bed now. You sleep too much."

"Leave me be, it's too early."

"Sun's been up near two hour already. You git yer'self down them stairs now. An' I want hair combed this mornin' an' face washed. No excuse for the way you been livin'."

How had she gotten away with this all these years? You'd have thought she was the mistress of Shadow Hollow with her demanding ways and sharp tongue.

"Elbows off that table," she said after I'd taken my seat in the dining room. "Yer momma's not here but that's no reason to act like bar-brians." She was close; we knew what she meant. The other two sat across from me looking about as cross as anyone can be.

"What are we going to do now?" asked Molly. She was pushing her oatmeal around the bowl, her head resting on her hand, her braids practically falling into her cereal.

"Eat your breakfast," I said.

"But I don't want to and you can't make me." She was seven, what could I expect.

"You eat it now or I'll get Nanny back in here and you'll be sorry."

"Leave her be Olivia. You're not the boss."

"Well Ryan-smart-britches, if I'm not, then who is?"

"Father is and he's not here." He stuck his

tongue out at me.

There was no answer that I could think of and besides I was tired of fighting with Ryan. I let him stick his tongue out all he wanted. I didn't care.

Nanny burst through the swinging door, as one broad hip pushed it open. She was balancing a platter of eggs and a pitcher of cider. "You eat up now, you hear. Miz Olivia you finish up and gwan' outside. Elijah, he be waitin' for you."

I wanted to say I don't want to and you can't make me but I didn't want to argue in front of Ryan and Molly or everything was going to fall apart.

Nanny plunked eggs and sliced ham on each of our plates. "Times a wastin' start eatin'." I looked down at the runny scrambled eggs. She knew I didn't like eggs like that. Now I was going to have to eat them or risk a mutiny at the breakfast table. Yuck. But we did as we were told.

Mother had been in the ground for only a week and we were still in a daze not knowing which way to turn, or what we should do or how we should do it. We had neighbors but they were so far away and we didn't dare leave the farm. Mother had no family that we knew of and if Father had left anyone behind in Scotland, he had never spoken of it.

As if reading my thoughts Ryan said, "How come we don't go get help?"

"Help for what and from who?" I asked.

"Well, there are people on the other farms."

"Yes, but there's no one close by and how do you suppose we'll get through if any of the soldiers are wandering about?"

Molly dropped her voice to a whisper, "What about Elijah?"

"And what about him?" I asked, unwanted anger erupting in my answer.

"The gun, and the Yankees."

"Who's to know? There's no one here but us and the slaves, and only Elijah and Nanny know anything about it. No one else needs to know."

"What if they find out?" she continued in her conspirator's voice.

I shot back with the same stage whisper, "They won't find out Molly, there's a war on. Why don't you know this?"

"I know that. Do you think I'm stupid?"

"Well now that you ask." For all the world, she looked like she was going to have a proper fit. And she did. She threw a piece of cornbread at me. Now that was so uncalled for and if Mother had only been here I know that child would not have seen the light of day for a week. Ladies, after all, did not throw cornbread, especially at mealtime. I pushed my chair back and left the table. One does not need to address every childish outburst, I decided. Ryan, who more often than not just ignored us, had no idea what to do next.

"Where are you going?" asked Molly in her very best whiney voice. Now she felt like she had the upper hand because I didn't go over and slap her for throwing that corn bread.

"I'm going to run a plantation."

Ryan's laughter followed me out the door. "You don't even know what a sheep looks like."

Last word was one of the things I was best at: "And neither do you Mr. I-know-everything." I slammed the door. It felt really good. In fact it felt so good I wanted to go back and slam it again.

Elijah was standing on the veranda shifting from one foot to the other. He ignored the slammed door. "Miz Olivia," he said, as he removed his hat, using his good arm. My back straightened.

"What is it Elijah?" His black wooly hair

was starting to show speckles of gray. There was tiredness written all over his eyes.

"There be lots to do," he said. He shook his head back and forth as though not knowing what to say next or where to start. His hands kept wringing his hat, pulling it one way and then another. I looked away and took in all the lands we owned. It went from an entire side of a mountain down into the valley. Our house was set a ways up the mountain on a gentle plateau in a clearing with a few of mother's fruit trees scattered about. Nanny had a small kitchen garden just outside the door and there was a much larger garden down by the barns. Father had built three barns and fenced huge areas for the sheep. Some of the fencing was made of neat whitewashed boards, but others were of saplings woven in and out to keep the sheep penned.

A splotchy fog drifted over the low lands and hung in the tops of the trees looking as though it wanted to lift but wasn't so sure yet of the day. The sun was a pale yellow ball hidden behind the mist. The barns stood in a field of grass, every blade sparkling with the morning dew. In the distance, there was the sound of the bleating of sheep. Odd how I'd never noticed that sound before.

"We start by teaching you to handle a gun," said Elijah. "Never know what's gonna' show up here and you be the oldest so it be up to you."

"That's fine," I said. "Tell me when and where."

"Now," he said. "We go now." And we did. There was no time to fetch my shawl, or put on my boots or find my gloves.

Elijah led the way down to the barns. He poked around in the pile of hay and pulled out a long barreled rifle. "Your pap have a gun in the house and we gots this Yankee gun that I hid," he said as he pulled pieces of straw off the shiny metal. "I get them loaded for you and tell you where they be."

Walking into the thinning morning mist, he led the way up a trail, one I'd never been on before. "Cain't do this out where we can be seen. We do this when there be fog and we do it at different times." He didn't have to explain much more. It wouldn't do to have a slave with a gun get caught by the neighbors, the Confederate troops or the Yankees.

"Need to stay away from them sheep," he said, as he set up our first target. "Don't take much to spook 'em."

My first attempt at handling a rifle was disastrous. Father had never allowed us to hold a gun, never mind shoot it. The noise alone was enough to turn a sane person deaf. It was so big and heavy and awkward, I wasn't sure if I'd ever do it right. On my first attempts I never even came close to the target, my bullets flew off deep into the woods.

We worked at it and clumsy as my hands were, within a week, with a sorely bruised shoulder and aching muscles, I was beginning to get the hang of it. Not only did Elijah have me shoot but I had to learn to clean the gun and reload it. This should not have been my job, but now it was. Most days and at different times, I would get the nod from Elijah and we'd hike somewhere away from the house and away from the sheep. Sometimes we would talk between gunshots. Not much though. He was all business and was never real happy trying to teach me about shooting. One day I asked how come he and Nanny Anna never had any children.

"Did...," he answered and then fired off three shots in rapid succession.

"Well, where are they?" I asked. He handed the gun back to me; the barrel was hot and smoking. His hat was pulled low making it hard to see his eyes.

"Gone." I'd had conversations like this before with Elijah and knew that when he decided he was done talking there was no way to get him to answer. We continued in silence except for the ear splitting bang of each shot. His face etched in dark stone, let me know he'd shut down. There'd be no more discussion. I had tread where I had no business treading.

After a few long weeks, about the time when the ringing in my head from all those gunshots wasn't quite so bad, he declared me a good enough marksman and told me I was all right to do it on my own. It was safer that way he said. Besides, if any Yankees came upon me, they were unlikely to challenge a girl with a gun, especially one that looked like she knew what she was about.

• • •

~ CHAPTER NINE ~

Elijah had started asking questions about the farm. Questions that started with things like "...it's shearing time, you think it be a good time to start?" Where was Father was all I could think.

"And Elijah, what would Father have done?" seemed to be my answer to most questions.

"Miz Olivia, he take a long look at the weather and a close look at them sheep and then decide."

"Well the weather seems fine," I said.

"We need to take a guess if it's gonna stay warm like 'dis," he said.

"Well is it Elijah?" Guess I was getting a

mite testy, what with the ringing in my head and all. Even with wool stuck in my ears, I still came away from our target practice with ears that buzzed through most of the night.

"By my calculations I'd say it'd be good to start in the next week or so."

"Show me Elijah," I said.

"What you want me to show you?" he asked.

"Well where are the sheep for starters?"

"Follow me." We climbed up a well-trodden path going along one of the fence lines. As we got higher, I could hear the sounds of their bleating. As we came over a knoll there they were. "That's only some of 'em," he said.

"And where are the others?"

"More pasture land further on."

"Why are they here?" I asked while looking over the backs of all sizes of the wooly animals. Most were white, just a few odd ones sprinkled about with black wool. Some were grazing; some looked up at us as if asking who were we? None stopped chewing.

"Switch pastures when they done grazing one, we move 'em to the next."

"Where are the herders?" I was beginning to feel like such a fool. I'd never been up here. I had no idea that our lands were so extensive.

"They be down repairing fences today. Gotta get the corral ready for the shearin'."

A hundred other questions came to mind, like how often do they shear the sheep and what do they do with the wool, but I was getting a bit sensitive about always appearing to be such an idiot. The most I knew was that we ate a lot of lamb, we wore wool all winter and Nanny had once said that our candles and soap came from the sheep. I had never thought much about that and would have to give some time to that last part.

"Elijah, where is my father?"

"Miz, I don' rightly know." He was looking over the backs of the sheep as if counting them. "They're nice and clean this year, not covered in mud like what happens some years."

"Where do you think he is?" I asked, feeling that he knew something but chose not to reveal it.

"Who?" Elijah could be outright stubborn sometimes and this was going to be one of those times.

"I want to know where Father is and I think you have some idea."

"Miz," he said, as he kicked at a tuft of grass, not meeting my eyes. "I left him in Frederick to catch that stage. That's last I seen 'im.'"

"Elijah, I know you have some thought as to what's happened. You can tell me. I won't tell anyone, there's no one to tell actually, but you must have some idea."

"Captured maybe."

"Captured by whom?"

"Miz Olivia there be a war on; who's to know. Strange things happenin' out there."

"Elijah," I said, "If one more person tells me there's a war on I'm going to flat out spit. Just out and out spit." One side of his mouth started twitching as if he was trying to control a smile. He turned away.

He knew more about Father, I could tell, but I knew that when he had nothing more to say there wasn't a thing that could be done to get him to tell what he didn't want to. Maybe Father had told him not to discuss anything with us. He had been a part of the farm since Father bought it all those years ago and would probably die for him. There was an unspoken agreement or friendship between them. One that I couldn't understand.

Curious as to why Father had left the farm in the hands of a slave, I began to question Nanny Anna. Her explanation was probably more than I needed to know but she started with "Miz Olivia, it has to do with that leg of his and I know no one speaks too much 'bout it. Think maybe they thought it best to keep it to theirselves, but I'll tell you what happen." She cleared her throat and poked at the fire trying to get it just right under the pot of stew.

"The way things is there's no harm in you knowin'." She let out a great sigh. "It happened when you was a little thing jus' startin' to walk. Only thing, you wasn't one to walk – you ran. Mostly to keep up with you' big brother. 'Tween the two of you it took some watchin' to be sure you wasn't off someplace you wasn't s'possed to be." Another great sigh and then, "One day when your pwas off chasing some strays and your Momma and I was in with the looms, you and that rascally brother of your'n were s'possed to be nappin'. Well we shoulda known. The two of you somehow got outside. It was early spring and dat river had overflowed its banks and was rushin' with all them broke trees and branches from the last ice storm, and that's right where you was headed."

She straightened up and put her hands on her hips, annoyance showing in her clipped speech. "Well sure 'nuf you was too young to know and no one's real sure exactly how, but you had somehow fallen into that river. You' brother screamed and screamed. He couldn't a been much more'n three or four. Your pap heard him and went tearin' down there. He saw the pink of your dress caught on a branch right smack in the middle of the river. It took some doin' but he got out there in that freezin' cold water and grabbed on to you."

Nanny shook her head and the worry lines on her forehead made it look as if she were living the whole day over again. "'Course the water was rushin' so fast and had gotten so deep from the snow melt up in them mountains, it was a whole lot deeper than your pap expected and 'course he couldna swim. Turned out it carried him down the stream. 'Course he wasn't gonna' let you go no matter what happened. You'd been screamin' so loud. Louder maybe than yer brother, what with the cold and all."

She drew in a deep breath and continued. "Elijah'd been movin' the sheep to a new field when he heard it all. He tore off like a mountain lion in search of a meal. He dove in that water – no matter that he couldn't swim neither, an' he git over to your pap who was holdin' you over his head so's you wouldn't drown. Elijah grabbed ahold a you and got you over to shore. Your pap's leg was caught between the rocks and he couldn't move and the water was rushin' so fast. It was an awful mess."

She took a breath. "Elijah figured your pap was a gonner. But he jumped back in that water and got back over to him. 'Tween them, they yanked and pulled and dodged the branches and trees that were rushin' through that water that was colder than ice."

"Somehow the two of 'em they got his leg unstuck. It was broke for sure. They hung onto some busted up branches that got them over to our side of the river. Elijah half carried and dragged your pap off that branch they was clingin' to. Your pap was half drowned." She drew herself up to her full height and continued. "To this day neither one of 'em says much 'bout it. Think the whole thing 'bout scared the words right of 'em. They was that scared."

She took a deep breath before she continued. "Your Momma and I had tore down there from hearin' all that screamin'. You was fine but sure look like we was gonna lose both yer pap and Elijah. Yer Momma and I had to wade in to drag 'em both out for the last bit – they couldn't hardly stand up."

A great sigh escaped. "We got 'em all back to the house and warmed up. It was as if your brother lost all memory, he never said one word 'bout it since then. He may not even 'member it happenin'." She scratched at her turban and smoothed down front of her apron, "My recollection is you' Momma and I rock you wrapped tight in a blanket the rest of the day. You couldn't stop sobbin' it had given you such a fright."

Poking at the fire for a moment, she turned and continued. "'Course that Doc didn't show up for two days and we had to set yer pap's leg. Wasn't perfect mind you, but couldn't wait for the Doc to get here." Her fingers tucked the wisps of hair that had escaped back under her turban.

"You' pap of course still has that limp. Don' think he ever wanted you to feel 'sponsible so that's why no one's said too much 'bout it. That leg only bothers him now and again I've noticed. But Elijah's savin' his life has kept them real close all these years. They rely on each other for jus' 'bout everythin'. They're tighter than ticks."

I had nothing to add and only wondered if that was why I'd never been too fond of swimming or even wading in the water. It was a lot to think about and I wondered how much Andrew remembered, as I'd never seen him down swimming in the river either.

I had a new respect for Elijah and went out to find him. I wanted to say thank you but wasn't sure how. He was moving a herd from one pen to the next, Fergus busy at his side. I wasn't sure how to even start a conversation to thank him for what he'd done. It seemed awkward so instead said "Let's get the shearing going."

"Cain't," he said, "too late in the day. If it be dry and warm in the mornin' we start then." He knew most everything and I at least knew not to argue.

In the morning, we started. Not that I was much help. The herders were skilled at shearing and it was a sight to watch them. Their shears came very close to taking off the entire coat of each of the lambs in one fast go round, their clippers slicing deftly between wool and skin. The sheep were docile leaning against the shearer once they had them flipped over. I was tired of watching. "Elijah what can I do?"

The herders seemed to have their roles well laid out. As one would grab an unsuspecting sheep and flip him practically onto the shearer's lap, the shearer was ready with his clippers and in no time had that sheep sheared. Then, the newly shorn sheep, shaking and not sure what had just happened, was pushed out of the pen. They would bleat their hearts out probably from the odd feeling of losing their coats. They looked so naked with their newly shorn bodies. They were as pink as a just bloomed spring azalea. Elijah was there collecting all the freshly shorn piles of wool.

"Here, Miz Olivia," he said holding out a large glass bottle. "It be tincture of iodine. Rub some on nicks or cuts you find."

"Yuck," I said, "How can I do that?" He ignored me and handed me a rag and the bottle of reddish brown liquid. "Don' miss none of them nicks or scraps," he said. "They get infected real quick if not tended to."

I took the rag and dabbed a bit of the rusty red iodine on the nearest scratch. The sheep didn't like it at all or maybe they just didn't like me or knew I didn't know what I was doing. Not one of them stood still even though I was trying to help them. Within minutes the rag was saturated with as much blood as iodine. I wanted to be sick and thought I was going to have to run around the side of the barn to retch, but I didn't want to appear to be so weak and fainthearted. I wanted to help and I guess this was where I was going to learn, even though this was not where I would have chosen to start.

Nearly half of the sheared sheep needed some attention. Sometimes there was a wound with open bleeding and sometimes just a scratch. It seemed that if they kicked up a fuss while being sheared they were apt to get nicked by the shears.

My iodine soaked hand quickly became accustomed to the sting and after a while didn't feel it anymore. By the end of the day I was sure we'd sheared the entire herd. "More tomorrow," said Elijah.

"There are more?" I thought surely we had sheared every living, breathing animal in the county. I wondered if I'd be able to even walk by morning. My arms ached, my back hurt and my boots were sorely pinching my toes.

The sun was nearly down when I reached the house. Every bone in my body was screaming for relief. I'd been bending and pushing and slapping that iodine on just about anything that moved. The front of my dress looked as though someone had bled to death on my lap.

Nanny Anna met me at the door. "Got a nice

warm tub waitin' for you in da kitchen," she said as she eyed me from head to foot.

"Too tired," I answered.

"No you not," she said pushing me in the direction of the kitchen. Molly stood in the dining room door, her mouth hung open, a look of shock pinched her face. I must have been a sight, and for once she had nothing to say.

Nanny Anna made quick work of getting me into the tub. She scrubbed my hair and then just let me soak in the warm water. I wasn't sure if I had the strength to get out. But there she was, "Come on, out you go." She pushed me up the stairs and I was tucked in with a bowl of soup and lots of warm bread before I even knew what was happening.

The next day it was the same thing all over again. By sunset, we had finished up. I helped Elijah stuff the last of the wool into the back of the wagon. "Now what?" I asked.

"We store some and wash some," he said. "Gotta get it to market."

"Where's the market," I asked.

"I bring it down da road a piece," he answered.

"A piece where?" I asked as I threw the last bunch on top of the pile, my arms aching in protest.

"Find a market for it," he said. "Sometimes one place sometimes the other."

I was too exhausted to play word games with him. Swiping my forehead one last time with the hem of my dress, I looked up to see a trail of dust rising from the road. The hoof beats of horses getting louder. Hoof beats that were heading in our direction.

"Elijah, run, quick. Hide." I could just make out the blue coats of the Yankees.

• • •

~ CHAPTER TEN ~

Where did the strength come from to run to the house? I have no idea. But bunching up my skirt I ran with all the energy that I had left. Every tired and aching bone protested. My feet wanted to give up and not carry me another step. Mother would have swooned had she seen me running with my legs and pantaloons out there for all the world to see.

The kitchen entrance was nearest and it was off to the side of the house so's the approaching horsemen would likely not notice one lone girl dashing for safety. I caught a quick glimpse of Nanny Anna standing in the window; she was holding something behind her skirt. I was nearly certain it was a rifle. For a moment I wondered what she was going to do with it.

Ryan and Molly stood inside the kitchen door. "You two, up to the attic, fast now, you hear?" My breath came in gasps. Ryan wanted to question, but looked at me and changed his mind. He followed Molly who looked scared beyond reason.

"Nanny Anna what do I do?" Why I thought she would know I have no idea.

"Go on out and talk to 'em, we got no choice. Maybe it'll keep 'em from comin' in the house. Elijah's out der', I jus' know he is. He got a gun trained on 'em from somewheres."

"But there must be twenty or more of them." I drew in a breath and tried to smooth down the front of my iodine soaked skirt. Nanny opened the door as the horsemen pulled up to the front stairs. She stood behind the door and gave me a push. Trying to stand tall, I stepped out onto the veranda I willed my hands to stop trembling.

A hiccup escaped. The fright and the run up the hill was just too much and I still hadn't caught my breath. I searched for my handkerchief to muffle the hiccups but it was soaked in iodine.

"Good day, Miss," said a soldier as he tipped his hat. He seemed very tall sitting astride his horse. From what I could see he had a short beard and reddish hair. I had to hold my hand up to shade my eyes. The sun was setting behind him creating a golden, reddish glow all around him. "I'm Captain Downing ma'am at your service."

Not at my service, you damned Yankee you, I thought but didn't say out loud. I smiled up at him with what I hoped was a charming smile and caught myself as a hiccup threatened to escape. There were so many of them, all mounted on a ragtag group of horses, all of whom were fidgety. I knew little of horses. This group may have once been well trained, but now seemed skittish and hard to control. They snorted and stomped about, none wanting to stand still. The soldiers looked like they were a long ways from their last meal and were too tired to much care what their horses did.

"Yes Captain what may I help you with?" Help you with indeed I thought looking up at him, but I continued to smile while holding my breath hoping I wouldn't make too much of a fool of myself in front of the Yankee trash. There was a light breeze that carried the soft smell of newly opened apple blossoms and for just a moment cooled the flush that I was sure had reddened my cheeks.

"Are you in some sort of trouble ma'am?" he asked. I was still a bit breathless from the run up to the house and for a moment held my fingers over my mouth trying to stifle the next hiccup. His eyes were inspecting the iodine stains running up and down the front of my skirt. I'm sure I must've been a sight between the blood like streaks and hair flying about in every direction.

"There are no problems that I know of; I was merely working with the sheep." I said trying to sound sweet. My thoughts were with Elijah hiding somewhere with his gun trained on the Captain's Yankee head.

"Ma'am, we'd like permission to spend the night down by the creek. We'll move along in the morning."

"You may spend the night," I answered trying to think of how on earth I could be rid of them sooner.

"And Ma'am, with your permission I should like to come to the house later and make the acquaintance of the owner." He didn't wait for an answer but tipped his hat again and pulled at the horse's reins. I turned back to the house just in time as a hiccup escaped. I could feel the red creeping up my neck as my face got hot. I heard his horse pause but I didn't turn around.

Nanny closed the door behind me. "What else could I have said?" My voice was trembling between hiccups.

"You done jus' fine," she said. My back was against the door as I slid down to the floor. I had to sit for a moment afraid I would fall over.

The sun sank behind the mountain as we watched as one after another of their cook fires was lit down by the creek. It gave a rosy warm look to the valley. Nanny and I peeked from behind the drapes watching as they set up their tents.

Our dinner was what was left of last night's lamb stew. We stayed huddled around the kitchen table, thinking that there'd be less of a chance of their seeing us. Nanny had gone out and pulled the kitchen shutters closed.

We were just starting to feel safe when there was a knock at the front door.
"Hide, quickly," I said pushing the two towards the morning stairs. It was the only escape out of the kitchen without someone seeing them.

"No," said Ryan, "I want to see one of them

up close."

"Oh no, you don't," I said and slapped him hard with the slap that he'd had coming for days. "Now git." Lord, I thought, I'm becoming like some common country trash. Ryan looked back at me with an angry scowl as he headed up the stairs.

Nanny Anna went to the front hall and opened the door. There stood the Captain. "What you want?" she asked, her tone less than inviting.

"If I might speak to the owner," he said.

"He not home yet," she answered. Good answer I thought, make him think he's just out for a spell.

"Then who is in charge in his absence?"

I went into the front hall. "I am. May I help you?" My manners had just plain flown out the window because I was not going to invite any Yankee trash into a home of mine. I stepped outside the door and stood there like some common trollop and crossed my arms. "What is it that you'd like?" Nanny Anna's eyes were about to pop out of her head with my brashness.

"Ma'am," he said removing his hat, "I'm Captain Downing."

"Yes, you'd said that earlier." He was at

least a head taller than I was and I was tall for a girl. His eyes were the deepest blue I'd ever seen and his beard, that wasn't very long, had a reddish hue. My face suddenly turned red when I realized how closely I had been observing him.

"I have some questions," he said, a smile playing at the corners of his mouth. He knew I'd been inspecting him.

"Well you just go on ahead and ask." I still was not going to invite him in. There was a smell of bacon wafting through the air and I could hear pans banging around at their campsite. A banjo player was plucking out a tune.

He stood there holding his hat eyeing me just a bit too closely. I certainly hoped this Captain wasn't thinking of being invited in for dinner. "Ma'am, we picked up what we think was a deserter awhile back, who had in his possession, two extra horses. Said they belonged to two men he'd been traveling with." He stopped a moment, "and said they were shot somewhere near here. Shot by a Negro slave. Would you know anything about that?"

"How on earth would I know anything about something like that?" I asked hoping my eyes held the look of wide-eyed innocence.

"Have you seen any soldiers or trespassers on your property?" he inquired.

"Captain we own something close to 1,000 acres. I cannot account for every soul that ever sets foot on our land."

"Then you're saying you haven't seen any shootings here by a Negro slave?"

"I have not." And I hadn't, they were shot dead before I'd even come out the door that horrible day.

"Well by all accounts it appears that they were deserters and very possibly dangerous. But we've been unable to find them." He paused, I'm sure he wanted to say more.

"I don't see how that would concern me."

"We were in the area and thought it would do no harm to check on things. Thank you then Ma'am, I'm sorry to have disturbed you."

"Well good night then, Captain," I said and turned back into the house. I could feel his eyes piercing my back. It gave me an odd tingling feeling. He didn't turn and walk back down the stairs until Nanny had closed the door.

We all spent the next few hours peeking out from behind the drapes to see what they were doing.

"Did they have horns?" asked Molly, her

face squinched up as if she didn't really want to know.

"Of course not," I answered. "They're just men like any others." My answer sounded so confident.

"Was he a Captain," asked Ryan, forgetting the slap I'd given him earlier.

"He said he was, but who knows," I answered.

"Gosh, I would have liked to have met him," he said.

Why, I thought. He can do us no good at all and it would lead to nothing but more trouble.

By morning they were gone. I can't say I was delighted. Maybe I was even a bit disappointed. But I didn't want to think about it.

Elijah came up to the house and told quite a tale. He said he stayed out of sight and listened to their conversation before they left early in the morning.

"Miz Olivia, they was gonna burn the whole place down. That's a fact. Heard 'em discussin' it."

"Why?" I asked, "Why would they want to burn it."

"So's the Confed's wouldn't use it for food an' such."

"What Confederates," I asked.

"Sounds like mightin' be some in the area."

"I wonder what kept them from doing it?"

"Couldn't tell 'cept that Captain said the farm belonged to Darcy McArdle and they weren't burnin' down nothin' that belonged to him."

"How'd they know that and how do they know Father?"

"It's by me," said Elijah who turned and walked away - a little too quickly. He was shutting down again and that's all I was going to hear from him. Nanny shrugged her shoulders and she too looked as though the cat had gotten her tongue. There was too much to do, and I didn't have time to go after a couple of slaves to see what they were being so closed mouthed about.

Nanny had pointed out that we were having another problem; we had very little food left. There were still a few chickens and we could eat all the lamb we could hold but there were only a few cups of flour left, a bit of sugar and cornmeal. She said the vegetables wouldn't be coming in for a month except for peas. "We'll grow some more," I had said.

"Not that easy Miz Olivia. Takes seed and

time."

Why didn't I know these things? Why did I have to wait until we were all starving to death to learn how to grow a cabbage? What was wrong with me? I had been eating three meals a day with tea in the afternoon, and never once questioned the source - where it all came from.

Something snapped in my head. I don't know why. But without any thought other than this was absolutely the last straw, I lashed out at Nanny. I was so worn out. I was so tired of everything getting worse and worse and nothing was getting better. I yelled at her and didn't really mean to be so heartless but there she stood, taking it all in as if she heard this every day of her life.

"I can play the pianoforte and can waltz a waltz with the best of them. I can conjugate a verb in French and in Latin. I know how many petticoats to wear and how to cinch a corset. What good does this do me? I can't shear a sheep. I have no earthly idea what to do with a pile of wool, and I wouldn't know how to harvest a carrot if my life depended on it."

My anger and frustration kept mounting. "How did this happen? Why didn't they teach us anything? Anything! Something useful. What can I do with all this useless, completely useless knowledge?"

I swiped at the tears running down that just wouldn't stop. Nanny Anna did a quiet "Uh huh," from deep down in her throat.

"So I know how to embroider and read music and I know all the great authors, but what am I going to do with all that? Would somebody please tell me?" I stamped my foot and used my sleeve to swipe at the tears that were dripping off my chin.

Ryan and Molly stood rooted to the spot, their mouths dropped open, not sure if they should laugh or should cry 'cause I had finally just plain out fallen to pieces.

"Yes," I said as I glared at them. "I am hysterical. In Latin that would be hystericus! In French it's hystérique! Use it as a noun or a verb, use it alone or go ahead and make a complete sentence out of it, whatever you like, either way it means pretty much the same thing."

Nanny Anna said something like this may be a good time to have a cup of tea or some such. I stomped out. What could they say? There was no answer. We had no money and I had no idea how to plant an ear of corn or any other food stuff and very soon we would all be going hungry. I left. I let myself out the kitchen door and just let it slam behind me, scaring what was left of the chickens.

. . .

~ CHAPTER ELEVEN ~

The weather was cool, it was spring, the prettiest time of the year but I hardly noticed as I made my way up the mountain path. I needed to think. We needed a plan and I had none. If we had money, I didn't know about it. And money was what we had always used for anything that we needed.

I followed one of the trails up Mount Ursus, my great mountain, and tried to bring order out of this chaos. What was I to do? Why did they all keep looking at me for a solution? How would I know the answers? I didn't.

Spring flowers had popped up everywhere. I'd never seen such a show of dazzling color with the blue of the now fading bluebells and the whites and pinks of the newly emerging azaleas and mountain laurel. Bluebells had been Mother's favorite. Her words pricked at my mind - she had said there will always be trials but we need to get past them. Well is this the kind of trial that she meant - that we were about to starve to death and I had no earthly idea how to get past that.

Thoughts of money spiraled through my head. Where? How? How do people get money? Sell something I thought, but what? I walked until my legs wanted to crumple beneath me. As the sun dipped below the horizon and twilight settled in, there was nowhere else to go. My feet led me back down the mountain into the coolness of the night that silently slipped down into the valley.

~

Perhaps there was something we could do. Perhaps there was something we could sell. If we could get Elijah to take that wool to market; it was going to be the only way. We were all going to starve if something wasn't done soon.

He had a plan but would say little. He knew

exactly what he was going to do but chose not to talk with me about it. Caution seemed to be uppermost in his mind as he made himself busy for a few days. He wanted to be sure that the Yankees were out of the area before he started anything.

When he seemed settled that they were gone, he pulled the wagon out of the barn ready to be loaded up with wool. We had washed it a few days before. Even Ryan and Molly had been pressed into service. There was no one else to do it. The sorriest part of the whole thing was that there really was no other help. Two of the herders had up and run away just before the Yankees had come and we had no way of tracking them. They were flat out gone. Two runaway slaves, what would Father say? The two herders who were left couldn't help with the washing 'cause they were busy tending the sheep.

Lambing was about to begin. I didn't want any part of it. I especially didn't want any part of looking like an Irish washer woman with my sleeves rolled up to my elbows, dunking my arms in the soapy water, while rinsing a pile of oily wool.

Nanny Anna had set out huge kettles of water that she warmed over the open fires. Like it or not, we took one batch after another and washed the wool in a soap that had been made from fat from last year's butchered sheep. My, I thought, the things I was learning, as I pumped my arms up and down pushing the soapy water through the wool.

After squeezing most of the soap out, we rinsed it and then put it on racks to dry. My hands were blistered from the endless squishing and pulling but they were soft from the lanolin in the wool. It wasn't quite the odious task that I'd imagined. The water was comfortably warm. Nanny said it had to be the right temperature or the texture of the wool would change.

Ryan spent the entire day grumbling about slave's work and Molly tried her best to keep up. By day's end we were soaked through from the splashing wash water. The wool was spread throughout the backyard on makeshift racks drying in the shade. Night came on us before we were through. The dew settled on the drying piles of wool, which kept them damp for an extra day. It was a relief when Elijah had declared them dry enough to stuff in the cotton sacks. The bags of wool were ready for market.

I asked Nanny to tell me about milk and cheese. "You get one of them sheep to stand still long enough you make yo'self some fine cheese."

"Well what about candle making and soap making?" Both, she said were made from parts of the sheep. Well what parts?

Here we go again I thought - trying to pull information out of a stone. But Nanny shared as much as she knew and I told her I wanted to start now. She eyed me as though I had told her I was about to walk to Boston. But by the next day we had a small vat of tallow bubbling on the fire.

"Gawd," said Ryan, a term he'd never used when Mother was alive, "What is that stink." He pushed the hair back out of eyes as he tried to get a better look at what we were doing.

"Oh Ryan, shut up." This was my new favorite term and I enjoyed using it, especially on big mouth Ryan.

"It be the fat," said Nanny as she came back out of the kitchen, a bucket of lye balanced on one hip. "Now jus' watch," she said. "You mix the lye in with the fat and it set up nice."

"Nanny, it does stink doesn't it." I said.

"Well now 'course it does. What you want it to smell like flowers?"

"That wouldn't be a bad idea." I said, not very seriously. "Why don't we crush up some lemon balm and add it to the mixture? We've got some dried."

"I know," said Ryan, "that's what Olivia hangs in her chiffarobe to make her things smell nice." He was taunting me. I wanted to give him another good slap but then we'd never get anything done. I ignored him and ran to my room for the basket of lemon balm that really did give everything a nice fragrance.

"Now you hold on a minute, cain't just go throwin' that in the pot. Crunch it up some and we sprinkle it in after we pour it."

It worked. It wasn't perfect, there were hunks of leaves that were too big but when we cut the bars, some looked very nice. There was a slight fragrance of lemon. And the dried leaves had colored the soap just a little which gave me another idea. Why not make it a pretty color?

Nanny would know what to use. I was so excited. We could sell soap! Try to sell it to the town women. We needed tissue to wrap it in and a bit of yarn to tie it up with and we'd have something as pretty and sweet smelling as anything that came over in the ships from Europe. If we could make enough of it, Elijah could bring it to Mr. Brown's store in town and they could sell it for us.

Elijah was ready to head to town to try to find a market for the cleaned and bagged wool. And so together we loaded his wagon with as much wool as it would hold and then added the few bars of soap that were pretty enough to sell. We watched as he made his way down the drive. There was a secret compartment in the seat of the buckboard where he hid a rifle. That was where he placed the six precious bars of fragrant soap that he promised to carry to Mr. Brown's store. There was no telling who he would meet on the way to market so had to be careful especially with the rifle. It would not be good for a slave to be caught with a weapon.

He still hadn't told me exactly where he was going but had said it would take him a couple of weeks to finish up his business. He was being closed mouthed again and I didn't have the time to question him. We needed to get back to work. The ewes would soon be dropping their lambs and we were shorthanded.

Elijah had said there's nothing to it. Just stand by and watch. Those mommas knew how to take care of their little ones. I'd never seen a lamb born before and was quite sure I didn't want to either, but quickly changed my mind.

After watching the first little one get born, I

wondered why Father had never brought us down to the barn to see it. The momma needed nothing. She delivered her own little lamb and then licked her baby until it stood on its own shaky legs and started protesting the mother's rough tongue.

My first baby lamb had pale pink skin and little tufts of wool scattered over her skin. And that was only the beginning. There were so many being born that for the next two weeks I don't think I left the barn. Even Ryan was pressed into service to carry down some food. It was almost easier for me to eat down there although a couple of times Nanny had come down and fussed at me so bad that I went up to the kitchen to have my dinner. She spent the whole time muttering, "What's this world comin' to? If your Momma could see you now settin' at this table, yer hair a sight, yer dress a mess, Lawdy, Lawdy."

I was tired. I hardly felt like eating and felt even less like being chewed out by Nanny. Change the subject I thought, just like we had done with Mother when she had us in the classroom.

"Elijah once told me you had children." I said as I stuffed a piece of war bread into my mouth. Nanny gave me a sharp warning look.

"Don't be stuffin' dat bread in yer mouth like some animal." It was actually pretty awful bread. Ryan had started calling it war bread because it was made from whatever could be scoured up, be it wheat flour, cornmeal or ground up oats. It was dry and tasteless.

"Well did you ever have children?" persisted Molly. Guess I knew when to leave something be. Molly still had a lot to learn.

"Did once," she answered.

"Well where are they?" I shot Molly a look but she ignored me.

Nanny was busy poking at the fire, her back to us. "Best if we leave some things alone. Best not to spend a heap of time mullin' over what coulda' or shoulda' been."

"But where are they?" asked Molly. Did those two know nothing about when to stop?

Nanny came over to the table. "Miz Molly, you want to know where my babies be?" She was cross and Molly was her favorite. In Nanny's eyes, Molly could do no wrong. But Molly had pushed her. She stood over us, her huge brown eyes angry and sad at the same time. It was almost frightening; I could see her tremble as she crossed her arms over her ample bosom. "Before yer pap bought us we live on a sheep farm way down in da Carolina mountains. Yer pap buy us at auction – Elijah and me. Someone else gets my boys." Her voice both deep and subdued had a catch in it.

"But how could they be your boys?" she persisted. "Weren't they owned by the farmer that owned you?"

"They my boys," she said. "You think they pulled them two babies out of the masta's body? Is dat what you think?" She was trembling as though from some great exertion.

"But," said Ryan, "You belonged to him, so did your babies. Didn't they? Papa said so."

"They my boys. They sell them 'fore they sold us. I borned those boys. They was mine." Her voice caught and she stopped for just a moment. "Don't know where they be now."

Her stare was piercing. "You three got anymore questions?" That was about as uppity as I'd ever seen Nanny, but guess that shut Ryan and Molly up for awhile.

This wasn't going to be a good time to stay around the kitchen. I tried to keep the door from slamming as I slipped out and made my way back to the barn.

• • •

~ CHAPTER TWELVE ~

Reuben sat on top of a bale of hay twining and untwining a length of string around his dark and work worn fingers. He'd been the herder who had been with us as long as I could remember. He had said it often calmed the momma some if someone was there. He was staying close to one of the sheep. I watched as that momma seemed to be having some trouble. Her eyes looked both sad and scared. She gave an agonizing bleat and Reuben, as calm as you please, reached over and eased that baby on its way. It was one of the largest lambs I'd seen and just needed that little bit of assist. The momma scrambled to her feet and sniffed at her new little one in approval. I had so much to learn.

This was just the beginning as one day blended into the next. The happy sounds of new little lambs filled the air. It was easy enough to sleep in the barn and Nanny Anna didn't get after me too badly. Who else was going to tend to them?

Our two herders Reuben and Big Ob were busy bringing the mothers and babies back to good pasture. Soon as they were a couple of days old they could be taken outside and brought to one of the fenced areas. Big Ob was escorting them down to the valley with its new spring grasses. "Only problem now," he'd said, "Are them mountain lions and wolves."

"Why is that," I asked, already sure I knew the answer.

"Like to eat them new lambs."

"Well what does Elijah do?" I asked.

"Shoot 'em." He answered.

Elijah came back after two weeks, just about the time the ewes had finished dropping their lambs. His cart was empty.

"Elijah, did you sell it all?" I walked along the side of the wagon, trying to get his attention. His face was grim; he pulled at the reins to slow the horse. Where was the other horse I wondered?

"We talk about it up to the house," he said. He tipped his hat and let the horse find his way back to the barn.

He met me in the kitchen. "Miz Olivia there be soldiers everywhere." He shuffled his feet and twisted his hat in his gnarled hands with their ragged finger nails. "I try all the different roads and trails. There ain't no way to get outa this valley."

"I don't understand the problem. You were taking wool to be shipped to the mills, why is this so difficult?"

"Cain't be done." He had practically torn his hat in two. "The Con'feds rob me of the whole load." I didn't even ask why he hadn't used his gun; I guess I was learning something about the ways of the world. "Tried different ways when I saw 'em comin'. They didn't catch up to me 'til jus' about half way across the state. Said they confiscatin' it for the cause. Took the other horse too."

Now what are we going to do I wondered.

"Elijah would it help if I tried to drive it to market?"

"Oh no, ma'am. There be lots a' bad people

out there and soldiers. You don' wanna go." He had stopped twisting his hat and stood in front of me, his eyes were reluctant to meet mine but he wanted to make me understand. "Them soldiers don' trust no one. I tell 'em it's jus' wool and they don' believe me. They stuck them bay'nets through them bags and poked around like they thought I be hidin' somethin'. Tried goin' to the west and was stopped again. There ain't no way we's goin' to get the rest of that wool to market this year. Not without yer pap here to do it. There's a war on you know." I wanted to stamp my foot and tell him that I was well aware there was a war on.

It all sounded very odd to me but I was learning and I knew things would be difficult. We were having another problem – all of our money was gone, the strong box that I had found and had been dipping into was now empty.

Nanny had informed me that most of the food we ate was grown right here on our farm. She also said we needed seed and then Elijah chimed in to tell me that some of our tools could no longer be repaired but needed to be replaced. Even I knew this was going to require money. Elijah said our credit at the town shops had about run out and Mr. Brown, although a friend of Father's needed his money too. As Elijah turned to leave he pulled a packet of envelopes from his pocket. "Picked 'em up for you at the post office Miz Olivia." I glanced at the pile. None of it looked good. He turned back once more. "And Miz Olivia, I near forgot. Mr. Brown, he say he buy your soap, but not for too much. He give me this." He held out six silver coins. "He say women not buyin' much with the war on, but said bring him all you got and he'll see what he can do." I looked at the coins. It wasn't much but a secret thrill snuck up on me as I realized I had done something that had produced some results and in this case results that could save us from starvation. The satisfaction that I had really done something worthwhile wanted to spill over, but I put on my serious face and said "well hopefully we can at least buy some seed with it."

~

The sun was setting, slowly slipping behind the mountains. The clouds were hanging heavy, as if waiting for the last of the light to be extinguished. We were going to be in for a storm. The air felt thick and expectant. The two herders had taken the last group of mothers and new lambs to the lower pasture. It was late, we'd had an early supper of boiled stew with some greens that Nanny had managed to find, part collards and part something else that I didn't recognize. That plus the cheese from the sheep's milk kept us from all starving to death.

Taking the lantern I headed back down to the barn. Nanny didn't question me for once; she was getting used to my comings and goings at odd hours. I wanted to look in on the ewes that were still in the barn. There were so few left thankfully, tonight I'd get to sleep in my own bed.

They looked up as I peered into the pens. Most seemed content with their mouths chewing in their endless motion. One ewe, smaller than the rest, seemed to be having some trouble. Her tongue lolled out of her mouth as she panted and paced around and around in the corner of the pen as though unsure of what she wanted to do. Her eyes didn't have the usual sleepy eyed look, but were looking about with a wide-open stare as if searching for help. I pulled open the gate and tried a few calming words as I grabbed a tuft of wool under her chin and a good handful of the new wool on her rump. I pulled her out of the pen and led her over to the stall. She started bleating as though I were hurting her but the look in her huge brown eyes said help me. Pacing first one way then another she stayed close to the walls, rubbing the sides of her huge belly along the roughness of the wooden slats.

"What is it?" I asked trying to use my calming voice. She stopped a moment and looked at me. I reached out and scratched at her new fuzzy coat. What could I do? She bleated loudly and I watched her stomach convulse. One tiny leg was emerging from just under her tail. She needed to lie down but she paced back and forth straining the slats that she leaned against. Her bleating was like a pleading. How to calm her?

It felt like hours that I'd been there. The storm that had threatened had started with all its fury. The wind had picked up and was smashing the rain against the roof and the sides of the barn. It made such a racket it sounded like gunfire. It wouldn't last I knew. It was one of those fast moving spring storms that scrubs everything clean and then moves on.

But it wasn't ending yet and the pounding of the rain seemed to make the mother more agitated. I had no idea what to do and there was no one to help. I had seen the herders flip a sheep over almost on their backs to shear them and so tried to pull her over. Reluctantly she came down on her front knees and I was able to push her over. Another leg to match the first one emerged. The tiny little thing was being born backwards. Lambs need to come out face first but this one was the wrong way. The momma cried and struggled to stand, her eyes with their long lashes pleaded with me. What could I do? I grabbed hold of the two little legs and pulled as hard as I could. I watched the mother. There seemed to be a rhythm to her pushing. I tried to get into that rhythm and as she would push I would pull.

Within minutes out popped the smallest lamb I'd ever seen. She wasn't moving, just laid there without an ounce of life in her. The mother looked over, her eyes large and sad, and then laid her head down. She was not going to be able to help this one; there was too much blood everywhere. I took up a bunch of my skirt and began rubbing her little lifeless form trying to mimic how the mother would lick their babies bringing them to life. She had tiny tufts of bits of black wool peppered over a soft pink body.

"Come on little lamb, you can do it. Don't you dare give up." I rubbed harder, all down her sides and ran my fingers over her head scratching under her chin and between her ears. "Come on little Black Rose," I said. "You have to survive, you just have to. Please survive." I was so worn out, so tired. I didn't realize I was crying as I massaged and pulled at that baby. My eyes were blurring and I couldn't see but then I felt the struggle for a first breath and felt the little legs kick out.

"There you are now." Tears were mixed with the laughter. "Look at you. You're fine." She bleated a strangled sound and I reached into her mouth and cleared out the debris. The next bleat was loud and clear.

She was going to survive. Struggling up on wobbly legs that looked unsure of their mission, she looked at me with her huge dark eyes and took a few tentative steps towards me. She fell but right away tried her wobbly legs again and got herself back up. Looking over at the lifeless body lying in the hay, she came to sniff my face and sink her nose into my hair. "Little Black Rose, I'm afraid you're an orphan." Her warm damp nose sniffed at my neck as she nibbled at my ear lobe.

"Come along now," I said. The barn was getting cold. I picked up the tiny bleating lamb and headed back up the hill to home. The rain was easing and I tried to keep her covered. She shivered a bit and I held her close. "You want your momma don't you?" Snuggling closer, her nose sank into my neck, sniffing at my hair. "I think I may know how you feel," I whispered into her warmth.

Nanny Anna looked up from where she was poking at the embers in the hearth. I let the door slam behind me. She didn't look any too pleased when she heard the hungry bleating of the little intruder.

"Nanny Anna we're going to have to take care of this one. She's lost her momma."

Nanny wanted to object but took another look and let us be. This poor motherless one was going to be all mine.

"Is there a nursing bottle somewhere," I asked. She was going to need lots of care if she was going to survive. And if there was a hole in her life where her momma should be maybe I could fill it. Maybe she wouldn't miss her so much if I fed her and helped her and cared for her. Maybe she'd find a way to keep living even with that big empty space in her heart.

. . .

~ CHAPTER THIRTEEN ~

All those envelopes that Elijah had brought home had been spread over Mother's desk for nearly a week before I remembered they were even there. Most were very official looking. Most from a bank in Frederick. Picking up one at a time, I tried to decide whether or not to open them. Stacking them neatly, I put them aside, whatever it was it could wait. But then such a surprise. There was a letter from Andrew. It was tucked between some of the larger envelopes. I hadn't even seen it. I must have let out a yelp because Ryan and Molly came running to see what was the matter. Ignoring their clamoring for details, I tore it open, thoughts spilling through my mind: come home Andrew, come home. There were so few words but I read it out loud.

Dear Mother and Father and family, (If he only knew I thought.)

I am well. I hope that you are all well too. I am writing this from a hospital in South Carolina. My wound does not seem bad and the doctor says I'll be back on the fighting front in no time. I hope everyone is well. I think of you often.

> *Your loving son and brother,*
> *Andrew*

That was it? That was all he intended to write? He was in the hospital. But which hospital? And was he still there? There was no return address and not even a date. The disappointment was obvious. I threw the letter down. We wouldn't even be able to write back. The other two stood there fidgeting, waiting for more.

"There is no more," I said and pushed them out the door. There were no other words for them and I was too worn to offer excuses or make something up.

My mood was black as I toyed with the other pieces of mail. They were all addressed to Father. I felt the envelopes. Was I hoping to find a cache of money? I knew better. But we were desperate. There was nothing left in the strong box. The few coins from the sale of my soap had already been used for seed. Maybe one of the envelopes at least held a check. The hopelessness was pushing me down. We had no way to purchase the things we needed to keep the farm going. And we were nearly out of everything necessary just to survive like flour and sugar and rice. And we were all looking a bit grubby with no fabric to purchase; we hadn't had new clothes in almost two years. My fingers wouldn't stop toying with the unopened mail.

I took the thickest and slowly ran the letter opener along the edge keeping my fingers crossed: let it be good news. It wasn't. I would have been better off to have left it.

The letter was from the Bank of Frederick. It said that Father was in serious arrears and that if some effort weren't made to meet the delinquent payments, they would take measures to repossess the house. Most of the words made no sense. But how could this be? We'd always had enough money or at least I thought so. My hand shook and I let the letter drop as though it were on fire. There hadn't been a payment in three months so they said. How could it have come to this? What were we to do? Where was Father?

"What's wrong?" asked Ryan. "You look as if you'd seen a ghost." Ignoring my command to disappear, he had stomped back in the room and was staring at me demanding answers.

"I don't know what we're going to do."

"Do about what?" he asked.

"We have bills due, Ryan. By the look of the rest of these envelopes I suspect we have a lot of bills due." I flipped through the rest of the envelopes thinking maybe I could burn them then they'd just go away and I'd never have to think of them again. Where could we possibly get the money to pay whatever we owed and be rid of this debt? Was that maybe why Father had gone to Washington? He must have known. He must be trying to get more money. But all I knew was that he wasn't here and we were and we needed to do something. But what?

Black Rose was bleating – she wanted to eat again. I'll tend to this later, I thought, and headed for the kitchen leaving Ryan to come up with his own answers.

I had been feeding my little motherless lamb from a bottle that Nanny Anna had kept up on a shelf high up in the back pantry. She said she'd forgotten it was even there.

Whenever I came into the kitchen I was greeted by the bouncing ball of soft wool who easily escaped from the barriers I had set up to try to keep her confined. Nanny fussed and fussed about her wandering around her kitchen so I had made an enclosed area with chairs, which didn't really keep her penned up. With Elijah's help we'd built a small fenced area outside the kitchen door. We had taken to keeping her inside only at night, but here she was having escaped yet again. We laughed when she'd butt us with the tiny buds on her head that she thought were horns. She'd chase us all around the kitchen nearly driving Nanny wild, which just made us laugh all the more.

"I'll take her out and put her in her pen," I said as I grabbed a tuft of her soft wool. Nanny was only too happy to open the door for us. Holding her tight, I led her out, but before I knew it she wrenched free and I watched in horror as her four little hooves clopped off in a dash, down towards the barns.

"Nanny," I wailed, "where's she going?"

Tears escaped – for why? I had no reason.

"Well maybe she don't want to be a kept lamb."

"But Nanny, she was mine. I delivered her, I saved her, I fed her." I swiped at the tears that wanted to embarrass me.

"Miz Olivia," she said, "There ain't no livin' thing wants to be kept. Every livin' thing wants to be free. You cain't change that no matter what you do or what you done did."

I looked at her and wiped the tears from my eyes. Her lips were closed in a tight straight line but there was a sadness and a sort of wanting deep in her dark eyes. I watched her for a moment and just for a minute I thought I could see stories behind those eyes, stories I'd never heard and my guess was that there weren't very many with happy endings.

I guess I didn't want to know more. "Come on," I said to Ryan, "We've got to do something and I have an idea. We're going to go find those spinning wheels."

~

The melancholy feeling that was over-whelming me wasn't helping at all. I could feel myself being pulled down into a place where I didn't want to be. I needed a plan or I was going to go to my room and never come out again. I wanted so much to crawl into bed and pull the quilt over my head and disappear. Let others handle the problems. I was only sixteen and this was not what I wanted for my life.

How could all of this have landed on my shoulders? Why had all these problems become mine to solve? I picked up my skirt and did one final swipe, drying my eyes. I stomped up the stairs not giving a fig how loud I was. Ryan, at a loss as to what to do next and sensing that I was up to something, followed close behind.

There was a loom in the attic. I had seen it. Ideas began to spin around in my head faster than the tears that I kept swiping at. We could weave cloth - if we could learn how to do it. It would bring a good price, better than sending the raw wool to market. The loom was still there, dusty, with parts that looked like they should be somewhere else besides piled on the floor of the attic. I tore back down the stairs. "C'mon Ryan, we can figure this out."

"Nanny Anna, how do you work the loom?"

"Miz Olivia, you cain't do that. It take too long and you be needin' lots a practice." She was busy wiping up the mess that little Black Rose had left on her usually spotless kitchen floor.

"Well you're going to teach me."

"These hands hadn't touched a loom in years. My mind hardly 'members." She scratched at her turban making it wiggle back and forth. "How you think you goin' to do somethin' like that? You don' know nuthin' 'bout looms."

"Nanny Anna you are going to have to stop sassing me this minute." I stamped my foot. "I'm gonna sell you down the river if you don't stop that mouthy talk of yours."

"Miz Olivia," she said, rising up to her full height and shaking her head back and forth, her arms crossed firmly across her chest, "You need to get somethin' straight. You cain't sell somethin' you don't own."

"What do you mean by that?" My hands were on my hips; I could feel my face getting red in fury.

"You hear tell of the 'mancipation Procla'mation?" Her voice was strong and clear as she looked at me, one dark eyebrow raised. She was going to have no problem staring me down. "Chile, you no longer owns slaves. I be here 'cause of yer Momma and yer pap. Dey treat us right all these years. We stays here 'til yer pap gets back, then we talk. Humph!" she said, looking a bit surprised at her outburst. "Now you wants help with that loom? By and by I'll see if I 'member anything." She turned her back and left the room. It was a long time before my mind could get around the words that she'd just flung at me.

~

By week's end we found most of the parts to the loom and had gotten them moved out of the attic. The dining room was going to be our new weaving room.

"Miz Olivia, there be lots more to it then just weavin' cloth. A lot more," she added mumbling under her breath.

"Would you like to tell me or do I need to keep guessing just how we're going to do this?" She looked pained. She fussed with her apron, adjusting it this way and that and then tried to smooth out some of the wrinkles.

"You gotta spin it first."

"What do you mean spin it?"

"Well Miz Olivia, it's all just a big pile of fluff right now, it be needin' to be spun into yarn or thread."

"And how does one accomplish that?"

"Yer pap had it done down at the mill. But back when he only had a few sheep yer Momma did it. Then when the farm got so big that's when he started sending it out to be done. Course," she added, "them Yankees burned down that mill."

She looked at me and shook her head. "There be too much here. You don' know how to do it."

"I can learn can't I?"

"Yes'm, you can, but it gonna take awhile."

"Do we have spinning wheels?"

"I imagine so – somewheres."

"Well we need to get busy finding them." She did not look pleased as she shook her head back and forth all the time mumbling under her breath "I don' know, I don' know."

It took some doing but between the barns and the attic we found what we needed. There were pieces everywhere and we had no idea if we had all the parts.

The sun had set and still we worked trying to fit things together. Candles were set up around the room so's we could work after the darkness took over. There were all sorts of odd pieces. I looked at the collection of shapes of wooden wheels and spindles and bobbins waiting to be filled and wondered how this could be done.

In exasperation I threw up my hands. "Make them work," I said to Elijah and Nanny Anna. "Whatever it takes."

It took days. We could hear them tinkering and hammering and talking back and forth. Elijah had to go to town twice for parts, which he said he couldn't make. It took an additional four days. It also took the last of Mother's jewelry to make the purchases. If Mr. Brown hadn't known Elijah the trade would never have taken place.

After far too long tinkering with the spinning wheels and loom it appeared that they were working, or so they said. Elijah had to fashion a new treadle for one of the wheels that he wasn't so sure of, but it looked to me like it would function.

With three spinning wheels and four of us including Nanny we should be just fine.

"Now Nanny show us how." She looked at me as though I'd lost what few wits I had left and shook her head. Without further cajoling she took up a huge hank of wool. We watched as her fingers began to remember the moves that she'd done so long ago as they manipulated the woolen fluff.

Was it the hum of the wheel as it spun round and round or the feel of the soft wool that was so enticing? It didn't matter; I wondered why we'd never done this before. Nanny seemed happy carding the wool with deft fingers that made long puffs of soft wool. Each of us had a job and she showed us how it was to be done. None of it would be perfect, I knew that, but it would be better than looking at sacks filled with wool that couldn't be sold or that would be stolen or worse, burned by the Yankees.

Nanny taught Ryan how to card when she fell behind and Molly with her small delicate fingers enjoyed picking out the bits of straw and debris and then carding it, making the wool soft and manageable. My job was the endless rhythmic spinning of the wool into long soft strands.

Nanny said we'd need help putting the weft on the loom. It was a job she just couldn't do. It meant another two days as Elijah rode off to our nearest neighbor to see if help could be loaned to us. Nanny Anna said some of the other slaves knew how to get the loom threaded. She had just never mastered that part of it.

But Elijah returned alone. He was so big and powerful. He held his hat between hands that were gnarled with age but probably had the strength of a giant. I'd seen Elijah's might but I also knew that he had the quieting touch of a mother as he gentled a new colt or calmed one of the sheep distraught by a storm. But now he seemed defeated. Elijah just shook his head. No help could be spared.

What had we done that people were now shunning us? Did they all know that Mother had died and that Father had not returned? Elijah had that look about him again that said he knew more than he was going to share. It was reason to wonder but there was so much to do. I spent little time mulling it over.

"I do it," sighed Nanny, "But it mightn't be right. It been far too many years."

"Nanny," I said, jumping up so fast I upset my stool. "There are books." Running out of the dining room, I headed down to the library and sure enough there was an entire section just on sheep and the profitable sheep farm. Nanny was breathless behind me, her bare feet slapping against the wooden floorboards.

"Cain't read dat," she said.

"I know that," I said. "But I can and you'll

know what they're talking about."

We did it. I read, she knew the names of most parts and when we got into trouble there were always sketches that we could look at to figure out how to do things. It took far more time than I ever imagined, but we did it. The loom was up and running. Sooner than we ever thought possible, our yarn that we'd so carefully spun into long strands was ready to be woven into cloth.

• • •

~ CHAPTER FOURTEEN ~

We cut our hair. Mine had trailed down nearly to my waist. Most times I wore it up in a bun, but it was always springing free in every direction. Ryan and Molly had straight blonde hair; mine liked to curl every which way and leaned towards straw color with streaks of blonde. That's how Mother had always known that I hadn't been wearing my bonnet, when my hair would get bleached from the sun. That and of course skin that some summers got so brown I looked like an Indian. But our hair had to be chopped off.

Suddenly there were troops everywhere. Nanny said we two girls had to be rid of our long hair so's to throw off any marauding soldiers. It seemed to happen almost overnight, that they discovered our existence. Considering that we'd spent the first years of the war all to ourselves, now it was as if there was a new roadway through our valley with soldiers wherever you turned.

We did get a glimpse of our first Confederate soldiers, anyways other than Andrew. Course that was the first thing we asked. "Anyone know of Andrew McCardle?"

We had allowed them to set up camp in the same place where the Yankees had camped. One soldier followed me up to the house and said yes, he thought he'd met someone with that name. He was a bit scruffy looking, his beard a combination of gray and dark brown, a scar ran next to his eye giving it a droopy look pulling down one side of his face, but we tried not to stare. We were so excited when he said he knew of our brother. We invited him in for a cold drink. Nanny watched us from the kitchen doorway and was giving me the most hateful looks. I told her to bring us all something cold to drink.

She came out of the kitchen, a tray of cold watered down cider balanced on one hip. "Ain't no lemons to be makin' lemonade," she said. Well we certainly knew that. And then to our new friend just as bold as you please she said, "Mr. Andrew always did love those lemon slices in his drink. I's sure that be what he misses most." Andrew hated lemons and she knew it. What was she thinking?

The soldier answered as he reached for one of Nanny's scones. "Truly he does. I remember it well." He had a thick drawl that spoke of the deep south. "That boy," he continued, "Would walk a mile out of his way if he ever heard there was lemons to be had." I looked at him realizing what Nanny was up to. She raised an eyebrow at me and left the room.

"Does he still wear that red undershirt?" I asked.

"Why yes'm he does. Wouldn't part with that for nothin'" he said while popping another scone into his mouth.

"Sir, I do believe we're not speaking of the same Andrew McCardle. I appreciate your time in speaking with us; we need to get to our chores." As I was speaking, I took his elbow and led him towards the door. "Good day," I said.

"But, but, but…" he began, as he stuffed one more of Nanny's scones into his mouth.

"But nothing." I said and closed the door behind him.

"That scoundrel." I stamped my foot. "How could he do that?"

"Miz Olivia, you don' want to be invitin' soldiers into yer house."

"Well I guess I know that now." Anger was seething over.

"Wouldn't go out and do them chores neither," she said. "Not with 'em all millin' around like that. Elijah's out there. He take care of it," she said as she cleared the glasses and wiped at the damp rings left on the tea table.

The day passed slowly. We'd been running free for weeks and now weren't comfortable being confined to the house all day and wanted to get outside. We were becoming accustomed to a new sort of freedom, one that allowed us to roam unaccompanied but sent us scurrying at the first sign of approaching troops.

We stayed in the house peeking out from behind the drapes now and again and sometimes we'd get a glimpse of a wandering soldier. There must have been close to a hundred of them camped down by our stream. They spoke in hushed tones. We heard none of the piped music and banjo strumming that we'd heard when the Yankees had set up camp. There was an ominous hush that seemed to hover over the valley, the air was quiet, the clouds were low and there was dampness everywhere. The smoke from their cook fires hung like a heavy grey fog over the valley.

The day seemed endless as we continued with our spinning and weaving. Lunch was dismal with yet more lamb stew without vegetables or any thickening. It was watery and filled with gristle. It was wearing on me. I was tired and sick of being confined to the house. I left the table unable to finish my soup and returned to my work.

Never in his life had Ryan done a lick of work without being cajoled and convinced that he had to do it and lo and behold before anyone knew what he was about, he had gone down to the barns, without our knowledge. He knew better than to be out there with all those soldiers. Why on earth he had done that could be anyone's guess. We were spinning our wool and waiting for him to come and help out, not knowing where he had gone off to. Where was he?

"Nanny, what is that boy doing now?" I asked.

Nanny liked to hum little tunes that

matched the strokes of her carding the wool, it broke her rhythm to answer me. "...no idea," she said, then tried to resume her rhythm as she pulled and raked the wool over the carding combs.

"Probably came back in and is up napping," I said, determined to catch him snoozing while we were all working.

Ryan was not in his room, or in the library, or in the kitchen. He was not in the house. That left the outside. If he was down checking the sheep, which he never did, it was taking a mighty long time.

There were over a hundred Confederate troops camped by the stream. They were there only for a day they told us, just to refresh their horses and give the men a rest. They had asked permission to slaughter a couple of sheep because the troops hadn't had fresh meat in weeks.

"For the Confederacy, Ma'am," said one of the soldiers. I saw no reason not to. In looking at them it wasn't hard to see they were all about starved to death. But where was Ryan?

It was coming on fall but not really cold yet, nevertheless I pulled on my cape and went out the kitchen door in search of him. It didn't take long to find him. He was in the barn talking with a soldier. I was so angry with him; I wanted to strap him so hard it would make Nanny Anna's punishments look like a walk through a clover field.

"Ryan, up to the house."

"You can't make me."

The soldier next to him stood when he heard my voice. He smirked and said "Now Ma'am, there's no harm done. We're having some conversation here nothing more."

"I said, Ryan, up to the house. Don't make me say it again." He gave me a hateful look. More than anything he wanted to join the army and who knows what they were talking about or what he had told them. Two other soldiers appeared from behind the horse stall. There was something in the air – it wasn't good, it was a tension. It didn't feel right. It was like a thickening of the air almost making it hard to breathe. Where was it that Elijah had kept that rifle tucked in the straw? I started to back up towards the pile of hay praying I'd be able to find it. He always kept it primed and ready.

"Now Ma'am," he said to me, "Where you goin'? Why don't you just stay with us for a spell and have some conversation." Words were failing me. I needed to keep them talking 'til I could get to that gun. I prayed it was there and that Elijah wasn't using it while he was up with the sheep keeping an eye out for mountain lions or wolves. Ryan looked unsure of what to do.

"Well y'all are doing a mighty fine job of protecting the Confederacy," I said trying to keep my voice from quivering. "We're right proud of you." My feet felt like lead as I continued to back towards the hay pile.

"Well, Miss, if you feel that way how 'bout a kiss for a soldier about to go back into battle?"

The soldier, who couldn't have been much older than Ryan, was coming towards me, his arm out ready to grab me to collect his kiss. The other two, considerably older, started towards me, both smiling, one with teeth so bad his mouth looked black. The other was dressed in what was left of what had once been a fine uniform but now was hanging from his body in near tatters. It showed far more of him than I cared to see.

"C'mon," he said. "Me and my friend just want a couple of kisses." He reached out for me. But I turned so fast he missed.

Please let it be here I said in a silent prayer and dove into the hay; let it be there my mind screamed as I snatched out handfuls of hay. My hand touched the cold metal. I yanked it out. "One step closer and it'll be your last," I said, my finger on the trigger. Oh thank you I said more to myself than anyone else. The gun had been there, but more importantly I now knew how to use it.

"Now wait a minute here," said the one closest. "We didn't mean any harm."

"If you didn't mean any harm you march yourselves out of this barn and don't come back." I clicked back the hammer for emphasis.

"Now you don't need to get so riled," said the one in the tattered uniform. "The boy wants to come with us. He wants to be the bugle boy."

"He's not going anywhere," I said, holding the rifle steady.

They shuffled towards the door never taking their eyes off me and the gun I was holding. They turned and were out the door, disappearing into the fading light. None had rifles with them or things may not have turned out the way they did.

"Now, will you go on up to the house," I said to Ryan, my voice nearly failing me.

"Olivia, you could've gotten us killed," he said, scowling for all he was worth.

"Well I'm not sure if that wouldn't have been a whole lot better than what they had in mind." I said. Ryan was dumb beyond believing. "It might be a good idea if we go to the next barn and hide out 'til dark in case they have any ideas of coming back."

Ryan didn't argue for once. We watched through a crack in the door until we were sure they were out of sight, he then peppered me with questions about the gun. I didn't answer but pushed him out the door. We crouched and half crawled and half ran through the field to the barn behind us. Nanny would just have to worry about where we were until it got dark.

It took forever for the last of the twilight to fade and then when I tried to get the gun back into the barn, sure enough, some of the soldiers had returned. We snuck back up to the house taking a long way round and came through the kitchen door. Molly, her little face pinched with worry, started to cry when she saw us. She was sure we'd been captured. And that was the night when Molly and I cut our hair. But there was more. We needed to look like young boys.

"There're enough of Andrew's clothes left for me to wear," I said. "And you can wear some of Ryan's. We can make them fit." I'd always wanted to try the freedom of trousers. Of course, my being tall, they seemed to fit well enough, except for the waist, but one of his belts took care of that.

It took those soldiers three days to leave. Three long days to do their damage.

• • •

~ CHAPTER FIFTEEN ~

Who's to know if we'd done the right thing chopping off our hair to look like a pair of young boys? We did it. Ryan nearly split his sides laughing. Molly loved her thick blonde hair but she stood like a statue as I went back and forth with mother's old sewing shears. She winced at the sound of each clip and tried not to cry when she looked down at the pile of white blonde hair piled up around her feet. It had to be done. We did it.

And then the sheep. Elijah had said to get them up the mountain before the Confederates set up camp by the river. He said there were just too many soldiers wandering around. Hungry, he said, all of them. We'd take them up later I told him, there was no need to be rushing about. So we had left them down in the lower pasture. Elijah walked away shaking his head.

When the Yankees had been here they hadn't far to look for their dinner and had taken only the few sheep that had been down by the barn. And, they had asked before taking them.

The Confederates had been another story. There were far more of them and they were hungry. Most were so thin they were stooped over. There was a haunted look in their eyes and their cheekbones poked out above scraggly beards. Many had no shoes. It was hard to imagine that what they were wearing had once been a uniform.

It still didn't account for what they did.

They killed most of the sheep.

We heard the shots and confusion and Fergus barking and the troops laughing and yelling and carrying on. We didn't want to be seen. We stood out of sight in the upstairs windows, trying to see down to the pens where the sheep were kept. We stood listening as the shots rang out, not able to see most of what went on. They had just plain out fired their rifles into the flock and laughed as one after another, with blood spreading over their white fleece, fell in place. They were packed so tightly that they fell against each other, not falling to the ground but held up by the others. The ones that were wounded cried pitifully. Why hadn't I taken them up the mountain? Why hadn't I listened to Elijah? I watched the little that I could see in horror until I could watch no more.

"What is the sense in that?" asked Ryan.

"They're doing it so's the Yankees don't get them."

We peeked out again from behind the heavy drapes and watched as they dragged and carried many of the slaughtered sheep down to their camp. The light from the fires and the smell of roasting meat was hard to miss. It wasn't too long before they'd run out of dry wood. That's when they came up to the barns and ripped off pieces of siding. We were glad that we had the sense to stay out of sight.

When they were done, they had roasted much of our herd and ripped off a good portion of the sides of our barns. The damage they did made it seem like they'd been camped there forever but it had only been three days.

On the fourth morning when I could stay confined no longer, I slipped out the kitchen door while everyone was sleeping. I was greeted by a morning fog that was just beginning to lift. It wasn't far down to the stream. Buzzards were circling; their raucous calls broke through the morning mist. My heart was pounding. I think I knew what I'd find there. Using the trees for cover I stood a moment to watch. Most of the soldiers had left with only a few remaining who were breaking camp and loading wagons.

I looked around. Were they barbarians? Two wolves on the other side of the creek eyed me suspiciously before they slunk off into the woods, their bellies extended to near bursting. The flies were choking the air with their buzzing. There were stripped sheep pelts thrown about like spit out watermelon seeds. They were stinking up the ground. There was offal and uneaten sheep parts fouling the stream. It looked like there had been a massacre. It was going to take days to clean the area and be rid of the garbage and putrid odor and pull the carcasses out of the water. There were fire pits filled with smoldering ash and bones sucked dry of their meat. The few soldiers who were left were doing little to clear up the mess, concerned only with packing up their belongings.

The fog seemed settled in the valley, parting

eerily to give glimpses of things best not seen. What could we do? It was beyond description. Following the stream down a ways, I took the long way back to the house trying to sort things out.

Everyone was up when I slipped into the kitchen. Ryan and Molly sat at the kitchen table munching what was left of last night's cornbread. They looked up as I entered.

"It's awful," I said. "I've got to get the few that are left back into the upper pasture. If I can get some out of there maybe we can save part of the flock."

"Should have let Elijah move them when he said to," said Ryan under his breath and none too kindly. Could I have felt any worse? It was like pouring salt into a wound.

"Miz Olivia, you don't want to be doin' that. Them soldiers'll shoot you if'n they catch you. Them thinking you're a boy and all."

"Who said they're going to see me." My feet wanted to drag, but I went and got Andrew's hat and jacket and pulled them on. They matched the olive green pants I was wearing. How nice, I thought, I'm in a matched outfit, maybe I could go to the ball.

I caught a glimpse of myself in a mirror as I

ran down the hall, then wished I hadn't looked. It was doubtful that even Father would recognize his daughter. My recently chopped hair had sun bleached blonde streaks running through it; it was a mass of unruly and close cut curls. My skin, that Mother had worked so hard at keeping a ladylike pale white, was now bronzed. I had grown taller or maybe just thinner, and try as I might, unless I kept my shirt bloused out it was hard to hide a chest that had been growing while I hadn't been paying much attention.

"I'll be back," I said as I silently slid out the kitchen door.

"Oh Miz Olivia..." That was all I heard before I pulled the door closed behind me. The morning was still gray with fine drops of cold mist swirling through the fog.

Stepping just a few feet from the door I realized this wasn't going to be quite as easy as I thought. The fog had gotten much thicker. We were all accustomed to the deep mountain mists but didn't often stray too far until it thinned out or cleared, and most times a morning fog would disappear as the sun warmed up the day. The bleating of the few remaining sheep gave some direction but still with the heavy air, the sound became distorted, giving a false sense of where it was coming from. It was easiest to take a few steps and stop and listen.

The barns were downhill from the house but so was the stream where the soldiers were camped. Moving with caution, it felt as though I was getting close and then I gasped as I heard two soldiers talking and laughing. They stood close to our old apple tree, relieving themselves. I had missed the path and was heading back to where they were breaking camp. I willed my heart to stop beating, sure that they could hear it through the mist as it pounded in my ears. They were so close I felt like I could reach through the fog and touch them. I backed away praying the fog would surround me.

But, it didn't. The fog cleared for a moment and one looked over towards me. "Hey," he said as he fumbled with his buttons. The other, much younger soldier looked over too, not in quite such a rush to button up. But then I'd forgotten, I was dressed as a boy.

I nodded a greeting and backed into the fog hoping it would surround me. Their voices followed me with questions, but I started to run. It was foolish; I couldn't see where I was going. Stopping I caught my breath and stood still to listen. The voices had stopped but the sheep sounded closer. Moving in silence towards the sound of the bleating, I discovered one of the fences as I nearly crashed into it. The gate would be over on one side. Easing along the splintery wood, it was simple enough to find it. I pushed it open and walked around the inside stepping around the few abandoned bodies still littering the ground.

There were just a few sheep still huddled together. They all look frightened. I had to get them out of there before the fog cleared or surely we would end up with nothing.

Sheep follow a leader. If I could get one of them to head up the mountain the rest would follow. Taking a chance I went to a large ram and grabbed a hand full of wool under his chin. Pushing with one hand on his rear end and pulling with the other wrapped in the wool, I separated him from the flock. He bucked and fought and I couldn't hold him and had to let him go. He turned towards me; head lowered, he pawed the ground and then ran right smack into me, butting me hard. His head felt like a load of bricks as it slammed into my thigh. Toppling into the mud, I was dazed for a moment. Trying to right myself, I looked up and there, staring down at me was Black Rose.

She'd grown so large since I'd last seen her. Her thick black coat had drops of moisture sparkling in the morning light. I was sure she remembered me. She sniffed at me in recognition then pushed at my hand to feed her and scratch at her head. I hugged her, my joy practically swallowed her up. She could be the leader.

Pulling and pushing and coaxing, I got her out of the pen. She jumped and bounced and tried to pull away, she wanted to play and run but already the others had started to follow her. Yanking at her with every bit of strength I had, I got her onto the path heading back up the mountain. Giving her a final push she took off up the familiar route, the rest of the herd following close behind.

"Mount Ursus here we come." I ran beside her as if we were playing a game giving her a push if she wanted to stop at all. It was a long hike and by the time we'd reached the upper pasture, the sun had burnt through the fog, lighting the forest with the fall colors, brilliant against the blue sky. I breathed a great sigh of relief as I watched Black Rose lead what was left of our herd into the pen.

The air was clear at the top of the mountain. Down in the valley the morning mist still hung like a protective blanket over the stream. It looked so peaceful. There was the occasional bird cry and two hawks high in the sky calling back and forth while enjoying the ride on the invisible currents of the north wind. I wanted to stay.

Taking a moment to breathe in the fresh morning air, I knew I had to head back down the mountain. Taking just another moment I looked over the flock. Maybe there were still enough left to begin again. I didn't know, I was tired. Tired of the whole thing. But I stood and watched for another moment and saw them all contentedly chewing their cuds and happily grazing on the last of the summer grasses. The fear they had in the lower pen was gone.

I turned and headed down the path. It took longer than it should have. The trees were glorious in their fall finery of crimson and gold. Leaves were falling, carpeting the path; it was hard to ignore the beauty of the day. It had drawn me in – I felt so free.

There was no warning, I heard nothing. How did it happen, how did I not notice? From out of nowhere two soldiers jumped out of the bushes right in front of me. I wanted to scream. My breath got caught in my throat; their guns were pointed right at my middle, their fingers curled around the triggers ready for whatever came. I wondered if this was it. Was this how my life was to end?

. . .

~ CHAPTER SIXTEEN ~

"Shhh," said the taller one holding a finger to his lips. The blue of his Yankee uniform had faded to an almost gray. "Not a sound, you hear?" He hadn't lowered his gun. I shook my head.

"Are you alone?" I shook my head again. "What are you doing up here?" he asked in a hushed whisper. I tried to deepen my voice and looked down at my feet feeling they'd know for sure I was a girl if they looked in my eyes.

"Nuthin'," I answered.

"Well now, chances are you were part of that rabble camped down by that creek. Why don't we take you back over to where our outfit is and see if the Major thinks you're up to "nuthin'."

The older of the two gave me a push forward. I shook off his hand and tried to take long purposeful steps. We were heading up and over the west side of the mountain, away from home and from where the Confederate soldiers had camped down by the stream. So they had seen them but maybe too late or maybe they were outnumbered and had chosen to stay out of the way.

We didn't have far to go before they pushed me into a tent crowded with men milling about. There was a makeshift table with a man about Father's age sitting behind it. Rough hands pushed me forward in front of him.

"What is it?" he asked, looking up for just a moment.

"Major," he said, "We found this here boy skulking around out in the shadows. 'Suspect he was part of that Confederate encampment."

"Well now, what would a young boy like you be doing skulking around?" asked the man at the desk, giving me a hard calculating look. "And I'd be curious boy, is there a reason you didn't leave with that ragtag group of Rebels?" There was quiet as all eyes turned on me. I shrank and willed the tears of terror not to fall.

"Don't suppose he'd be spying now do you?" asked the soldier.

"That could be a distinct possibility," said the Major. "Take him as a prisoner; we can't be too careful. I'm sure they've got spies all over these woods."

I gasped and I suppose the shock showed in my eyes. I looked down quickly not wanting the Major to see my horror.

"We're about ready here," he said as he slammed his book closed. His pen went skittering across his makeshift desk. "Get these things packed up and we'll be on our way."

It was as fast as that. One minute I had been coming down the trail from the mountain and the next I was in irons in the back of a farm wagon. There were two others in chains. Two horribly dirty men. One had only one eye and the other was missing half of his leg. Neither had shaved or had their hair trimmed in years, and the stench told me they probably hadn't bathed since the war began. They had little to say and chose to sleep for most of the way. The road was long and bumpy and we didn't stop until well after noon. What must Nanny think, what about Molly and Ryan? No one had seen me leave in the fog.

Looking off the side of the wagon as we bumped along, I thought how much I had always wanted to see what was on the other side of the mountain and now here I was. The only thing on the other side of my mountain though was a bunch of damned Yankees.

~

The winter snuck up on us. One day it seemed that the trees were draped in all the brilliant colors of fall. Now all that was left were bare branches that looked like the dark fingers of a long dead skeleton reaching into a cold sky. It had gotten so frigid that snow had begun to dance through the air like bits of dust, settling nowhere.

It felt as though we had been traveling for weeks, stopping only to set up camp and then hastily moving on. We met up with enemy fire only twice, both times we were left in the wagon with no protection had there been a stray bullet.

One of the prisoners had died after a week on the road. The leg that had been cut off had festered so badly and he seemed to be in so much pain that most times he wasn't even conscious. After they took him away there were only the two of us and we were ignored. My wagon mate said almost nothing; he seemed to be in another place, spending the day curled up in a tight ball in his moth-eaten blanket.

"Get on down here, boy," yelled a Yankee as he pointed his gun at me. Now what, I thought, not caring anymore what they did with me. "Over here," he said pointing with his rifle. We were at a train station and he shoved me into a building that resembled a crude barn with boards that didn't quite meet, leaving gaping spaces. The cold and wind blew right through. There were other prisoners but no one even looked up as the guards pushed us through the door.

Climbing over bodies, trying not to step on legs and arms, I settled into an unoccupied corner. They left us there for three days. Each meal was a wrestling match to get to the food. I moved quickly and was successful in grabbing at least a potato and sometimes a half loaf of bread. I carried it back to my corner, eating quickly before anyone could take it from me.

It was forever before they loaded us into the big empty freight cars of the train. I had curled up in a corner next to a very old man who snored loudly and was nearly blind. He hadn't noticed me until the third or fourth day of riding down the endless tracks. He introduced himself as if we had just met for a cup of tea.

Extending his hand he said, "How do you do, young man, I'm Old Man Charlie, 'tis a pleasure to make your acquaintance." For some reason it made me laugh. I shook his hand. All these fine manners in a cattle car where we were stuffed in like bales of hay. He didn't wait to hear my name but rolled over and went back to his snoring.

The train rocked and clattered and sped up and slowed down. I could see through the cracks in the siding. The cracks that let in the cold air but did nothing to let the fetid air back out. The landscape slipped by as I watched through the spaces between the boards. It changed from the forests to the open plains and then acres of untended fields with bent and broken corn stalks. Much of the land looked dead or abandoned. Heading into the sunrise, the train was taking us further and further away from home.

My mind strayed often from the dizzying effects of no food or water. Hunger and thirst were my constant companions. I had visions of never again being allowed outside to breathe the fresh air and enjoy the freedom of moving about. There were days when the train hardly moved at all, that was when I heard rumblings about the Confederates having blown up parts of the track. It must have taken weeks to get where we were going, from the ride in the wagon to the endless ride on the train. I had long ago stopped counting the days.

When it seemed like the trip would never end, the doors slid open with a huge bang. Yankees with guns trained on us stood waiting. It was hard to imagine how they could think we would give them any trouble. There wasn't a healthy or sturdy body among us. Some of the prisoners were missing limbs, some with dreadful, putrid wounds that were never going to heal and many with coughs that kept us up through the long nights. There was no threat from these prisoners.

One by one we dropped off the train, not sure if our legs remembered how to work. Single file, we were led to a line of farm wagons that would take us to our final stop, a prisoner of war camp.

The wagons were stuffed tight with bodies everywhere, but they all seemed beyond caring. As we jumped down from the wagons, Old Man Charlie, who had declared himself my protector, led the way. He seemed to know something about the routine and took us to a far corner, away from the mainstream of prison life. We had a long way to walk to the outhouse but there were fewer men in our little corner down by the water. It was only a thin line of sand that separated us from what he said was the Potomac River, a nearly endless expanse of open water.

Twice we had to move the torn piece of canvas that was called a tent when the water rose and lapped at the ground where we were sleeping. Some nights it was so cold I snuggled up to Old Man Charlie's back, sure I was going to freeze to death if he didn't let off some of his warmth. We had each been given one blanket but it was hardly enough.

Old Man Charlie had the strength to keep us alive on the train but now it was my turn. His one good eye had clouded over and his voice was nearly gone. I took care of getting us each a bowl of watery soup or a piece of moldy bread whenever the food wagon came through.

"We're in Point Lookout. It's way south in Maryland," he said in answer to my blank stare. All that traveling and we hadn't even left Maryland. "It's one of the worst prison camps known to man," he continued. The coughing took over and he had to stop talking. "I've been here before," he said when the coughing subsided. That was as much as he was going to tell me.

There was little that I could do for him as time dragged on, one endless day after another. "Charlie," I said, "I want to get them to take you into the hospital." His breathing was so labored, I was sure each breath would be his last.

"No," he said, the effort of that one word sent him into another coughing fit. "You ever see anyone come back out of that place?" He was right. We'd never seen a prisoner return to camp who had left on a stretcher.

Charlie slipped away one night just before the morning light brightened the sky. I probably wouldn't have noticed until daylight but the snoring stopped suddenly and that was it. I was sorry to see him go; I guess I was sorriest because it meant someone else would take his place in our canvas shelter.

They didn't replace Charlie with one prisoner. They replaced him with two. If it hadn't been so cold and rainy I would have moved out into the open just to be alone. I played dumb, as though my mind was gone and had little speech in me. They left me alone. However, a week later a guard walking down the rows and rows of tents shouted out, "McCardle, where the hell are you?"

With a voice that could barely croak from disuse and not sure I had heard correctly, I answered. I was beyond caring about what happened next. Anything would be better than living for even one more minute in the squalid conditions.

"Move." The Sergeant dug his fingers into my shoulder and then pushed me forward. The guard walked me across the entire prison ground exiting at a gate and then walking across a huge open area to get to a brick building that looked cold and stark against a grey sky. There seemed to be no reason why they had picked me out of the camp. It could not be good.

I stood in front of a makeshift desk, planks stretched across old barrels, their staves long past their usefulness. The room was dark, no windows and only the crude desk and two rickety chairs. My knees wouldn't stop trembling. Why had I been called in? They were saying that a prisoner exchange had started but the only prisoners we'd seen leave were the dead ones.

"You are prisoner number 8329?" asked the

man seated behind the desk. One lone lantern with a low flame gave little light. I couldn't see his face but I could see his arm. A huge bandage was wrapped from his wrist all the way up to his shoulder. A red bandana held it close to his body. He was unconsciously favoring it by rubbing at it every now and again.

"I suppose so," I answered.

"Hmmm, why don't you know that?" he asked, barely looking up from the scattered pile of papers.

"I wasn't assigned any number." My voice wasn't much more than a whisper.

"Well I'm here to interview all of the new internees as they like to call them." He laid down his pen and leaned back in his chair.

"You mean prisoners?"

"Yes of course that's what I mean."

"Well I'm not new. I'm sure I've been here over six weeks."

"I'm sorry," he said. "Apparently they're unable to keep up with the incoming prisoners. Do I know you?" he asked, leaning forward and staring hard into my eyes.

"I'm not sure, Sir," I answered. For just a moment I looked a bit closer at the man sitting in front of me. I lowered my head. I think I knew this man.

"Where are you from?"

I hesitated a moment. "Maryland, out in the Blue Ridge area." My words were mumbled.

"Speak up, boy," he said. "What is your business out there?"

"We're sheep farmers." He got up and as though an idea had suddenly dawned on him, he came around the table and walked right up to me. I could smell the warm wool of his jacket and a faint scent of soap. He turned to the soldier standing guard at the door.

"Thanks, Sergeant," he said. "I can take it from here." He stared at me so hard I had to look away. The soldier closed the door behind him. Everything started to tremble and I was afraid I was going to cry. He stood with his good arm cradling the one in the sling as he walked around me, first one way and then turned and headed the other way, his boots thumping with each step. For a moment I thought I saw the beginning of a smile but I quickly lowered my eyes again.

He stood to one side, and scratched for a moment at his beard. "And you say your sympathies lie with the Confederacy?" he asked.

"My allegiance is with the Confederacy, Sir,

mine and my family's."

"They have your name listed here as Orin McCardle. Is that correct?"

"More or less, Sir."

"More or less what?" he asked as he paced back and forth. "Tell me your father's name?"

"His name is Darcy McCardle."

"Darcy McCardle now is it? Hmmm."

He walked back around the desk and sat back down, wincing as he jarred his bad arm. "Who is in your family?" he asked.

"Who?"

"Yes, do you have brothers and sisters?"

"I do."

"Well then, tell me who exactly."

I sighed. I wasn't sure what his point was and I was tired of standing there being inspected by the likes of him. "I have a sister and a brother." He didn't need to know about Andrew.

"I thought there was another sister."

How would he know that? "There was."

"What's happened to that one?"

"She's no longer there."

"And where is she?"

A tear rolled down my cheek. I wished it away and tried to tuck my chin further into my shirt hoping he wouldn't notice.

"Would you sit, please?"

I didn't know what he was going to do with me next or if this was some sort of mean trick but I slid over to the chair and eased into it.

"I believe I knew your father," he said. "Darcy McCardle was supplying wool and food to the Union. I had dealings with him while I was in Washington. I hope he's well," he said. "I haven't seen him for the past few months."

I wasn't sure if he heard me gasp.

The shock at what he was saying must have shown. I could no longer look down but looked at him straight in the eye. "My father would not supply Yankees with wool, or with anything for that matter. You are mistaken, Sir."

"Oh not at all," he said. "Not only did he supply the Yankees with wool but he kept up a good supply of meat going to our troops."

"That is impossible."

"Your father's sympathies have always been with the North. He unfortunately lived in a divided state and in an area whose sympathies most decidedly lay with the south, but that didn't change his stand. He was a Yankee through and through, he just didn't talk about it."

What could I say? No wonder Father said

little about the war. No wonder he was so upset when Andrew joined the Confederates.

"Miss McCardle," he said. I gasped again but he ignored it. "We need to get you out of here." Another tear almost unnoticed slipped down my cheek. I stared at him unable to answer, not trusting my voice.

"We have been interviewing the prisoners to find informants. We can release a few. I will tell them you have cooperated."

"I cannot accompany you," he continued, "much as I'd like, as I am a friend of your father's. With this arm I am confined here for another thirty days. You've been arrested as someone supplying the Confederates with food and clothing. I can handle the details back here but you'll need to find your own way back to your home."

I looked at him still unable to speak. It was him!

He was thinner and his beard was longer, but I remembered him from when he had camped at our farm with the Yankee troops. He was the one who had prevented them from burning down the house and all the barns. How could I have forgotten? His name was Captain Downing. He had the bluest eyes and they were taking in all of me, from my tattered trousers to my nearly shredded jacket. I shifted uncomfortably. That smile was starting again around the corners of his mouth.

"I will have you accompanied to the livery. I assume you can ride."

"Yes," my voice was a croak.

"Do you know how dangerous it is out there? Do you have any idea?"

"Yes," I said again.

"I will give you money to get you home. I have a map that may help, but for heaven's sake don't get caught with it. You must travel at night. I will try to get word to your manservant so's he'll know you're coming and can maybe meet you somewhere. I suggest you stay in the outfit that you're currently wearing and be very weary of soldiers. The Confederacy is rapidly breaking up. There's lawlessness all around and it's extremely dangerous. Do you think you can make it?"

This time I shook my head unable to speak.

"Here now, take this." He came around from behind his desk and with his good hand, pressed a few folded bills and what looked like a faded map into my hand. "Keep it well hidden."

He bent down to my level for a moment and

looked at me again and then there was a full smile, showing very white teeth. His smile crinkled up his eyes. "Well done, Miss McCardle, I'll be looking for you at the end of the war."

"Sergeant," he yelled. "This prisoner is free to go, take him to the livery."

• • •

~ CHAPTER SEVENTEEN ~

It wasn't far to the ferry that Captain Downing said would take me across the Potomac. A few days following the river north and there it was. He'd said it would take days, maybe even weeks off my trip home if I avoided the northern route, the one over land.

I'd never been on the water before and the thought frightened me, but looking at John Henry, I knew we were going to have to take any shortcuts we could find. I wasn't sure just how far this old horse could take me before he was going to give up. He favored one leg and scars crisscrossed his grey body, but he was gentle and patient with me.

For two days, I waited on the edge of the woods, waiting for the water to calm. I nearly gave up and was ready to set out for the long ride north when I spotted what looked like an old man guiding a rickety looking raft across the river. Not wanting to draw attention to us, I stayed hidden in the trees, willing John Henry to remain silent. We waited in the shadows until a wagon and three men had gotten off and had plodded out of sight. Only then did we dare to come out of the woods.

John Henry trotted patiently by my side. The pilot of the craft looked up as we approached. It wasn't an old man at all, but a skinny old woman who had a pipe clenched tight in her toothless mouth. The pipe wasn't lit but she continued to puff on it as if there was a bowlful of the finest tobacco.

She said "nope, not leaving 'til tomorrow." That's as much as she'd say when I inquired if she could take us across. There was no arguing with her and besides I didn't want to attract any attention. I took the leather reins and led John Henry back into the woods. I was nearly ravenous from hunger but feared showing myself in case I was seen as an escaped prisoner. Again I slept with my stomach making loud unnatural noises. John Henry seemed content to graze nearby.

In the morning I approached Harriett, as she told me she was called. This time she said we could go. "Haven't eaten there in awhile have ye now?" She eyed me closely. "Here take this." She handed me half a loaf of bread and some cheese. It took no time to eat it and I thanked her only when I'd finished the last crumb.

Looking at me from head to toe, a twinkle came into her eye as she smiled her thin tooth-less grin. "Best keep that hat pulled low and that jacket buttoned up. You almost had me fooled." I grabbed at my jacket and pulled it closed using the two remaining buttons to fasten it. She laughed and continued sucking on her pipe. "Here, put these on him so's he don't get spooked." She handed me a pair of blinders for John Henry's eyes.

The crossing was smooth and with his eyes covered he hardly even flinched. I had buried my head in his side, sorry she didn't have a pair of blinders for me.

I had not told Captain Downing the whole truth. I could ride, but not the way he intended. We had never been allowed to ride either bareback or on an English saddle. We had been raised on a sidesaddle. It took little time to learn however and wasn't this what I'd always wanted to do? To ride free over the mountains. Riding astride, I discovered, was just a matter of get on and ride. It would take a bit to not be so sore at the end of the day however.

The horse that the Captain had made available must have long ago been retired from the Army. He was slow and awkward. There was none of the fluid motion of our geldings. But he would draw less attention with his slow and sometimes clumsy gait. It finished off the picture of just a farm boy in tatters riding down the lane.

Before the day was out I was stopped and asked what my business was. The five Yankee soldiers who surrounded me looked close to starving. "Have ya got somethin' to eat," begged one of them. I had nothing. There was no way to find food, no towns, no farms, no people.

"Look, I have nothing, only my saddle."

"Whyn't you with the troops?" one of them asked. Which troops I thought – I don't even know which side I'm supposed to be on anymore.

"Needed at home," I answered.

Their eyes narrowed as they looked me over, suspicion clouding their eyes. They had more questions but I was done answering. I flicked the reins and rode on, not daring to look back. I was going to have to be more careful. If I rode down any of the well-traveled roads I would have to do it close to dark, when I would have the chance to disappear into the woods. The Captain had said to ride after the sun had set but I didn't know the road and had already ridden off in the wrong direction more than once.

The first few days had been so tiring. The Captain's map pointed me northwest after coming across on the ferry, but I wasn't really sure that I was traveling on the right road. There were days of frigid rain and cold as I wondered if I'd ever be warm again. At the end of each day as I slid off John Henry, my legs would shake so that I could hardly walk to collect wood or take care of my business in the woods.

I had been gone from home for months and I needed more than anything to get settled somewhere. John Henry, however, couldn't be rushed and we plodded along at his pace. I had gotten used to my horse and he'd gotten used to me. Each night as I slid off his swayed back, I would be a little less sore.

The days were getting longer; the smell of spring was in the air. The coolness of the evening was settling in and the sun was slipping behind the tops of the mountains. I thought for just a moment I could smell the violets of home. We were passing yet another sprawling farm; I heard the bleat of a lone sheep, a wave of homesickness swept over me. It was a new feeling and one that made me want to gallop the rest of the way, stopping for nothing.

Were any of our sheep left? Had Father made it home? Would Ryan and Molly survive without me? It seemed too far to go.

My mind was wandering from tiredness or hunger, I don't know which, but I never even heard the two men who came out of the woods. Before I even saw them, one was on each side; hands grabbed the horse's bridle and were dragging us into the trees before I could get my wits about me. I yanked on the reins trying to throw them off but they cursed me loudly and pulled all the harder. My only chance was going to be to run. Sliding off John Henry's back, my legs sore and stiff nearly failed me as I hit the ground. With legs unused to anything but clinging to the back of a horse, I willed them to run.

The worst looking of the two came after me.

I could hear him huffing behind me. For someone who looked so big and clumsy he certainly was fast. He grabbed the back of my jacket and threw me to the ground. Scrambling on hands and knees, I tried to get away. The last thing that I felt was his hand slapping the side of my head so hard that it nearly snapped my neck. That's all I remembered.

When I next opened my eyes, my arms were tied behind me to a tree. The ropes were so tight they were cutting my wrists. The two men, and by the look of them they were probably deserters, were cooking up a meal of the last of my bacon and my last few pieces of bread. It had taken the few coins I had left to buy it from one lone farmer who had almost nothing but was so glad to have what was left of my money.

The two were filthy beyond belief, remnants of blue uniforms hung in shreds from bodies that showed far too much. They were laughing and drinking something that was brown and that smelled like father's whiskey. They hadn't built up the fire and it was very dark outside the campsite. I needed to get away. My only chance was going to be to somehow get my hands out of the rope that they'd tied to the tree. I watched in silence as they drank, emptying the bottle and smashing it into the fire. The ugly one that had thrown me down and slapped me struggled up and staggered over for a better look. He leaned down to my level. The stink would have stopped a stampede of buffalo.

"What's my young boy up to?" he asked. "Got yer'self a big bruise there I see." His smile was not friendly; it showed broken yellow teeth and cracked lips. His eyebrows were so thick and bushy that I could almost feel them against my cheek. I turned away. He slapped me again, just for good measure I guess. It brought tears to my eyes. His hand was nearly as big as a dinner plate. "Nice soft cheek there boy. You must be mighty young." He started to pull off my hat, my cheek stung and tears were threatening to spill over.

"Hey Al, you eatin' tonight or what?" His friend called over from the cook fire. I could hear a couple of tin plates banging and smell the bacon that was making my stomach do somersaults I was so hungry.

"I'll be back pretty boy, you just wait right here for me." He smiled again, it made my skin crawl. My hands were fast becoming numb from the ropes. I was sure they were swelling up and I'd never get out of the ties.

"Could you give me a minute to pee?" I asked, using my very best deep voice.

"Sure, little boy," he said, "Just don't be going any further than the tree."

Looking around I tried to figure which way I could run. He untied the rope and held one end wrapped around my wrist. "Can't do it with you holding the rope."

"Sure you can," he said. "Bet you go like a girl." I turned away. He let the rope slack.

"Al, you comin' or am I gonna feed the bears this here food?" In the instant that he turned to his friend I yanked the rope out of his hands. I lit out for the woods, my feet crashing through the underbrush. I tried to undo the rope, but everything kept getting caught and tangled. The woods were so dark I ran into trees and pine branches ripped at my face. It didn't matter; I was going to get as far away as I could.

I heard the one called Al roaring in anger behind me. He sounded like an entire company of troops chasing me. He was screaming things at me with words I'd never heard before. Gathering up the rope, I ran blindly, hoping there weren't ravines to tumble into. Stopping for a moment to listen, it sounded like he was still running but not right behind me. Ripping at branches of a pine I reached out to find the trunk in the pitch black. I grabbed hold and scrambled up from limb to limb trying to be quiet. Course he was making so much noise he wouldn't have heard me anyway. The night was so dark he could've stood in front of me and probably wouldn't have seen me. I just had to stop breathing so hard and stop my heart from pounding so's he wouldn't hear it.

He stopped just past the tree and turned and yelled. "Jim where you at?" We were so deep in the forest he couldn't see the light from the fire anymore. I couldn't even see it from high in the tree. "Jim" he yelled again and then cursed loudly.

"I'm here," came a distant answer.

"Can't find you, keep yellin'." I listened as he stumbled along in the blackness of the night on his way back to camp.

Where to now, I thought? The night was so dark. There was no moon and only distant stars. I needed my horse and I needed the blanket. It was cold already. There was only one way to do it. I was going to have to go back and get him. Luck was with me. I set out in the direction that my kidnapper had taken and soon could see the faint glow from their fire.

The snores from the two were like a beacon, better even than the red coals. The noise guided me to them. The fire was low; an occasional snap of a burning twig sent sparks like fireflies shooting into the air. John Henry was tied to the tree, his head down as he nibbled at the bits of grass. The two deserters were in such a deep sleep there was little that would wake them. Nevertheless I crept from one tree to the next and watched as the big one named Al rolled over to make himself more comfortable. He burped and passed gas and after a few minutes resumed the even rhythm of his snoring.

John Henry's old tired eyes saw me but there was no recognition. Reaching out, I untied the leather rope, thankful that they'd been so lazy, they'd left him saddled. Leading him back through the darkness, we found our way to the road. He plodded very quietly as if knowing we were on a mission. We trotted off, our pace slowed by the blackness of the night.

After all those endless hours spent at home in that close and uncomfortable classroom, I finally found something I could use as I looked up and found the stars. There was Orion twinkling behind us over the eastern horizon giving us direction.

We rode through the night moving westward, wondering if we were getting any closer to home. We hadn't covered that much ground when light began to filter through the trees bringing a brilliant sunrise; it was a signal to us that it was time to get off the road. We didn't need another encounter. If the road continued west we could follow it all the way home. The Captain's map showed that it would bring us right into the northern tip of the Blue Ridge.

It was decided that this would be the way to travel. It would be slow but chances were we wouldn't be seen. Traveling at night we would move into the woods only when we heard or thought someone was about. By dawn each morning, John Henry and I would find a place at the side of the road to spend the day.

Our plan kept us safe and undiscovered, but it had gone on for too long. I was hungry and tired and needed to find food. The few ears of corn that I found in old fields were close to inedible; nevertheless, there were usually a few kernels that could be chewed on.

The mountains ahead seemed familiar and if the road was good we might be able to make it by next morning. I had to get there. I had eaten all the bread and cheese and even the stale and moldy piece of hardtack that the men who had captured me had left by their fire. There had to be somewhere where I could find something besides stale hard corn to eat.

We had pulled into the trees yet again. My blanket was smelly and itchy but it was warm and felt good to wrap up in as the morning light pierced through the trees. Changing to sleeping during the day hadn't been that difficult. I was starving and so tired I didn't care.

~

Where had they come from? They were all around me, the gray of their uniforms easy to see against the dark backdrop of the trees. It looked like there were hundreds of them. They were heading south. Most were on foot. Some on horseback. They were everywhere. I rubbed the sleep out of my eyes. My only chance was going to be to mount John Henry and maybe if we moved really fast, maybe I would survive to one day tell my grandchildren about my great escape during the height of the Civil War.

Mounting a fidgety horse wasn't one of the things I had mastered but clumsy as I was, threw myself up in the saddle. I yanked at his reins and dug my heels into his sides. He surprised me with his speed, but I guess I surprised him by slapping him hard with the reins. I hadn't done that before and he bolted.

I heard the shots before I felt the one that slammed into my leg. John Henry reared up and pawed the air; I felt myself slipping and tried to wind the reins around my hands. A pain shot up and down my leg like a thousand bees all stinging at once. There was a patch of red spreading across my thigh, soaking my trousers.

"Ride horse, ride," I yelled into his ear. My leg stung so badly I thought surely I would pass out and fall off in the road and be trampled to death. "Ride," I yelled again in his ear. I whipped him with the reins, while trying to stay mounted.

There seemed to be some long forgotten memory that came back to him of how he had been in his younger days. He took off at a breakneck gallop. The roadside became a blur as he flew like the wind. His hooves made such a pounding racket I couldn't tell if we were being chased.

It was easy enough to let John Henry decide which way we should go. I hung on scared that I'd fall or that the blackness would take over and I would faint away from the pain. We rode at racehorse speed for what seemed forever. As we wound our way into the hills his pace began to slow, his sides heaving, his dark body soaked and dripping both blood and sweat.

Blackness kept appearing before my eyes. I thought it must be night again as I slipped off the saddle. I dropped onto the floor of the forest. Pine needles cushioned my fall.

• • •

~ CHAPTER EIGHTEEN ~

The pounding in my head was threatening to split it open and my leg felt like it had been sliced apart. The mattress stuffed with dried moss crinkled as I moved one arm, willing my eyes to stay closed. I didn't want to know where I was. A cool smooth hand touched my forehead smoothing back my hair. I winced and shrank back.

"Mon Petite you are safe. Tell me now, how do you feel?" It was a gentle voice, husky - maybe from disuse. My lips formed the word terrible, but no sound came out.

"You will be better soon. You rest then and I will bring you some bouillon in a bit." Her accent was heavy but pleasant. I could hear the rush seat creak as she stood and moved away.

That same hand touched my shoulder sometime later. "Here now, I have something that will help with the pain." I forced my eyes open. The room was dim; it looked like the inside of a warm cave. There were shadows dancing about from the flickering of the flames in the fireplace. The person attached to that quiet hand was sitting on a stool next to my cot.

"Where am I?" My voice was barely a rasp.

"Up here in the hills, have no fear Mon Petite, you'll be fine." Focusing on the form sitting next to me, I could see a gentle face, almost pixie like, framed with white crinkly hair that was flying about in all directions. It looked like a huge halo surrounding her face. She was small and wore a comfortable dress of coarse homespun cloth in a pleasant rose color. Neither old nor young, she had smooth skin with warm pink cheeks.

"Try this," she said. Her voice was soft but husky, somehow not fitting someone so small. "You will like it I think." Slipping another pillow behind me, she spooned in a warm dark liquid with pieces of all sorts of wonderful things floating in it.

"Mmmm," I said.

"Well child, it should be mmmm. I think you have not eaten in three or four days. Now slowly sil vous plait, there is more where that came from." I tried to sit up. A pain shot through my leg.

"Non, non, you cannot do that yet. It will be a few more days."

"Where am I?"

"Here in the mountains. You are safe Mon Petite, there is no need for you to worry. I have never had visitors here. We are alone for sure."

"How did I get here?" I tried to talk while taking gulps of the wonderful soup.

"La cheval," she answered. She spooned in another spoonful. "Poor horse," she said. "The wound was too much for one of that great age."

"He was wounded?"

"Mais oui," she said. "The bullet, it went through your leg, it stopped in his side. A lot of blood. I did what I could."

"Who are you?" I asked.

"They call me Lara, although that is not my real name. My name is French and far too diffi-cult for the American tongue to get around." Her smile was hesitant, as if unused. "I stay to myself here in the hills. In the village they call me Mademoiselle de Fleur, the flower lady."

"Am I near the Blue Ridge?"

"Not so far," she answered. "Sleep now, you will need to get well."

It was morning when I was awakened by the happy crow of a rooster announcing the arrival of another day. The sun lit up the entire inside of the hut. I watched as pieces of dust floated about in the sun's rays that streamed through the two tiny windows. Shelves, bent low from the weight, were tacked up on three walls around the room. They were filled to bursting with different shaped tins and glass jars holding dried berries and mushrooms and nuts and dried flower petals. Bunches of bound together plants hung from the low rafters filling the space with a warm fragrance.

"Ah, there you are," she said. "I have eggs and some greens for you and a bit more of the broth if you are able."

"Oh yes," I said, embarrassed at the rumblings of my stomach.

"Here then," she said and placed a tray in front of me. "You are looking a bit better this morning."

"Thank you, and thank you for caring for me." I was wearing a snow-white flannel gown and it seemed that most of the dirt and grime had been washed off me.

"My chemise," she said. "It is a bit small for you but it is better than the outfit you arrived in."

"And what am I eating?"

"Ah, Mon Petite, there are a bits of collards from last fall and a few herbs floating about and a bit of chicken. We need to have you get strong again if you are to continue your journey." She didn't ask but the question was in her eyes.

There was no need to pretend I was a boy anymore. "I was captured by the Yankees at my home," I said, trying to be matter-of-fact. What's done is done, I told myself. "They put me in a prison camp down on the Potomac. I was let out and was trying to make my way home." I looked at the kind face watching me and willed the tears not to fall.

"There were a lot of Confederate soldiers and I tried to get away. They must have thought I was a spy." She put the soupspoon back in my hand that had slipped to the floor.

She shook her head in sorrow. "I am sorry Mon Petite. This a beautiful land, room for everyone. Why must they work so hard at destroying all that is here and everything that has taken so much effort to create?"

At least she didn't feel that she had to tell me there's a war on!

"I need to get back to my farm. My father has disappeared and my brother is in the hospital." There was so much ahead of me. Where to start?

"Ah, such a shame. I am sorry, I will do what I can to help you to mend but it will take a bit of time and patience."

Gunfire started far off in the distance. My spoon dropped again, clattering on the floor. "It is alright, no need to worry," she said, as she retrieved my spoon. "I have heard this before, but it is far away. They have been close but they will not come up this high."

She took my tray. "Indeed it is too sad," she said. "They cannot seem to see what is right in front of them. They have created such a mélange - a huge mess. There is a pall hanging over this land."

She paused a moment and stared out the window at the trees waiting for the warmth of the spring to open their leaves. "I wonder how they will go about the business of cleaning up what they have created."

She shook her head, then slipped into her

native French. I could follow only part of what she was saying. My French was limited to conjugating verbs and learning the names of things we could see in the classroom.

A quiet companionship began as the days turned into a week and then two. Finally she gave her permission for me to try my leg. "It went through the muscle, you must be careful; you do not want to injure it again."

The first day it was a few painful steps and then over the passing days the distance grew further. As she changed the herb infused poultice once again, she said there was no infection and that I was going to be just fine.

"I will need to go to the village soon," she said. "It is spring and the women will be looking for their flower seeds." Dried bunches of all sorts of plants hung in quiet disarray from the rafters. "I harvest the seeds of marigolds and athrium and nasturtiums and take cuttings of geraniums and trade them in the village for flour and salt and the few things that I cannot grow." She smiled, "The ladies do love their flowers out here in the wilderness."

"But how do you survive?"

"Oh so nicely. I have my vegetables and my chickens and my herbs and there's more than enough if one is careful. The goat gives me milk and cheese."

"Why are you up here?" I asked, wondering if perhaps I was overstepping with my curiosity.

She slipped back into her French, uncomfortable with the English she had adopted. I was able to follow most of what she said. "The world was suddenly too crowded for me. When I heard the first gunshots of the war, I knew it was time for me to find my patch of quiet. There is no peace in being a witness to man's inhumanity to man. I have found contentment up here with my flowers and the changing seasons and the serenity that nature provides."

I wanted part of that peace. It would have been very easy to slip into a companionship with this quiet person. My feet felt as though they were sprouting roots here in this warm and uncomplicated world. I did not want to turn towards home. Home - where there would be too much work and too many problems and I was sure there would be new sadness awaiting me.

I had missed it, and now the truth of what was ahead was settling in. Did I really want to go back to all those problems and the constant struggle just to survive? I was so tired of the never-ending trials for the barest of subsistence.

This was where I wanted to be. Here with this quiet person tucked up away from the difficulties of trying to survive and with the endless effort of getting through each and every day.

She must have read my thoughts. We were standing in the dabbled sunshine at her workbench filling tiny cloth sacks with flower seeds. "Child, you need to go." She was labeling the sacks with her careful penmanship *Forget-Me-Nots*. "You are too young to live the life of a recluse. There is much for you to do out there. They will be looking for you."

"I can't, I don't want to, I'm tired." I rubbed at the back of my neck and tied up the last of the seed packets.

"You have been the most wonderful companion and I shall miss you greatly but I fear they may need you more." Quiet light blue eyes were looking into my very soul. "Your farm with all of the animals I'm sure is a wonderful place to be and I think you did well to hold it together."

"It may not even be there when I get back."

"Oh I'm sure it will be and I'm sure they're waiting for you. Tell me more about your home and about your people." I had said very little before, only that we lived far north in the Blue Ridge and we raised sheep. It took a minute to bring up the picture and then to try to tell her what I was seeing.

We had been conversing in French for so long that I slipped in and out of her native tongue easily. I tried to explain how vast the lands were. And I spoke about how so many of the sheep were killed because I hadn't moved them when I should have and that I felt I had let Mother down for most of my life and then how Mother died needlessly. Some of what I tried to say just stuck in my throat and wouldn't come out.

I tried to tell her about my sister and brother and Nanny Anna and Elijah and how they'd once had children of their own. I said that someday I would like to help them find their children. I told her how my father had left and he didn't even know that Mother had died. I told her about Black Rose, the little lamb that I had helped deliver, but then she'd struggled for her freedom and I'd had to let her go.

There was so much more too, the weaving and spinning and how someday I wanted to learn how to make cheese and candles and how I was learning to make soap. And now that she'd introduced me to mint and lavender and rose petals, I could make more soaps to sell.

When I was done speaking, I wiped away the tears that had been blurring my vision.

~

This time there would be no horse, I was going to have to walk. Lara knew enough of the area to head me back in the right direction. Together we fashioned a pair of trousers and patched up Andrew's old jacket so it was serviceable. My hair was growing, flying out in all directions. We tied it back in a short ponytail and put on one of Lara's big slouchy hats.

"Do not forget, Mon Petite, you are strong, you are stronger than you think. You can do great things. You must remember," she said, her blue eyes ripping through the shell that had protected me these many months. "There is only one thing to do when we fall, and that is to get up and go on with the life that is set in front of us and to try to do all the good of which our hands are capable."

She pushed back a wisp of hair. "Et Mon Petite do this for all the events that come into your life and share your warmth and good works with the people around you." She sighed, "It is all we can do."

She patted my arm and for just a moment held that arm as if there was a moment when she would not let me go. But her hand slowly fell away. "You will make it to your home, it won't be long."

Adjusting my pack, she looked me over yet again. "Yes, that will do," she said. "Now off with you." I turned quickly, pretending I didn't see the tears in her eyes, my own clouding my vision. "Bon voyage my friend, we will meet again."

~

There were bluebells up and down the side of the mountain. The warmth from the spring day was comfortable. My feet were tired and my leg was beginning to ache. I was going to have to rest soon, but first I would finish my journey.

Nanny Anna was the first one that I saw, or she saw me. She had a hand up shading her eyes. I could tell she was squinting trying to see who it was coming up the drive. Her hand fell to her mouth, I could hear her saying over and over "Lawdy me, Lawdy me, she's not dead." I don't think I'd ever seen Nanny Anna run and there she was half running and half hobbling with her bad knees down the road, a cloud of dust rising up behind her.

"Child," she said, folding me in the familiar warmth of her arms. "Child, we thought you was dead. Hallelujah."

There was the scent of home that hung on her like a protective blanket as she buried me in a huge bear hug. I swiped at a tear as she released me. We couldn't seem to let go of each other as she pulled me along the drive and led me up the grand staircase to the veranda.

It was all here, the smell of comfort and safety, of mint and rosemary and sheep lanolin and the smell of apple blossoms about to burst open. And I was sure that I could smell the scent of our hearth when it's first stirred up in the morning with the anticipation of a crackling fire to come. It was just as I remembered it. Except for the man sitting in the rocking chair.

"Oh no." It came out as a gasp. "What's wrong with Father?" The wicker chair moved effortlessly back and forth. Bits of sand crunched, marking time with each backward motion.

"Miz Olivia, he been like dis since he got back." Her speech was slower than I remembered. "Seems he lost his mind. 'Tween losing your Momma and yer brother, his mind don't want to accept it."

"My brother?" My mind raced, "Andrew?" It didn't want to settle on any one thought. I didn't want her to put into words what I knew was going to be true.

"Oh Lawdy," she said, and began to wring her hands in her apron. I stared at her but her voice failed her, tears hung on her lashes, wanting to spill over. I looked more closely; she'd lost so much of her comfortable bulk, what had happened? Her hair, which had once been a lustrous black peeked out from under her turban. There were now streaks of grey that were springing free of their constraints. Puffiness ringed her dark eyes.

"Nanny Anna," I started, "how are you doing?"

"Tolerable," she answered, as a lone tear spilled off her lashes and left a trail as it slid down her cheek.

My feet felt like lead as I walked towards Father, the length of the veranda seemed endless. Like a blind person, my hand reached out to touch the wicker chair. "Father, it's me, I'm home." His eyes followed the sound, but there was no recognition. "It's me, Olivia." He shook his head and waved me off.

Nanny was close behind, wringing her hands in an apron that no longer had the crispness of earlier days. Our eyes met and she shook her head back and forth,
the lines in her forehead deepening.

"Well then," I said, "Where's Ryan and Molly?"

"They be comin' up in a minute, they down wif the sheep."

"The sheep?"

"Yes'm, they be droppin' their lambs pretty soon now. Those two be down tendin' to them. They be tryin...'" her voice trailed off.

"Molly and Ryan?" I asked.

"Well and who else is goin' to be doin' it? They been doin' it all, ever since we lost you. Seems Ryan knew a whole lot more than he let on. We didn't know if you be comin' back so those two, they get theirselves busy an' started to care for what's left of them sheep. Elijah been helpin' 'em out. They all gonna be mighty glad to see you," she said.

The sun was beginning to burn off the thick fog that had settled in the valley. It would lift I was sure before much longer. I looked up at our house. It was going to need painting; we were going to have to find some help for that. Father would need extra care. Maybe, with time, we could return him to who he had been.

The distant bleating of the sheep drifted through the air. That's when it came to me, I was home. This was where I belonged. Between us, we would get the farm up and running and back to where it once had been. It was going to take work and time, but somehow we'd get it right again. It was going to be a wonderful farm. We would raise sheep and sell wool and make soap and candles and grow crops again. Together we could do it, I just knew we could.

THE END

ABOUT THE AUTHOR

Tecla Emerson was born in Lexington, Massachusetts and went on to live in Boston, Plymouth and other towns in the New England area. Currently living in Annapolis, she is the publisher and editor of *OutLook by the Bay*, a regional magazine. She is the author of other young adult books to include *The Letter, Antietam, Waking the Fury* and *Jennie Wade: A Girl from Gettysburg.*

ANTIETAM - WAKING THE FURY

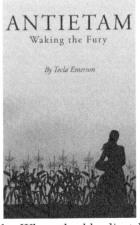

Emily at 15 is bored and annoyed with just about everything and everybody. Tired of her chores and irritated by the endless care of three younger sisters, she would like to have a life of her own. Her parents are absent; her Father is off fighting a war she doesn't understand and her Mother has left for Pennsylvania. As the eldest of the four sisters, she must take responsibility for her home and family. When the bloodiest battle of the Civil War is fought almost on her doorstep she is unwillingly pressed into service. Emily is called on to make decisions and to take charge of wounded soldiers while fending off the invading troops and protecting her younger sisters. Life changes forever as she discovers a courage that she did not know she possessed. Strengths emerge as she stands up for her beliefs while sheltering the enemy and caring for a runaway slave, both of which hold very serious consequences. In this remarkably accurate depiction of the Battle of Antietam, a legend is once more uncovered. It involves a mass of very angry bees. This dangerous, stinging swarm may well have had an influence on the outcome of that fateful day in 1862.

Now available at Amazon, Apple, Nook, Kobo and other online retailers in print and digital editions!

THE LETTER

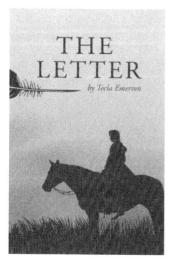

"My being forever banished from your sight..."

Just who was this "...undut-iful and Disobedient Child" who in 1756 penned a letter to her father in England?

What had she done to so offend him?

Why, as an extremely well-educated young girl, had she become an indentured servant? Why was she alone? In her letter, she pleads with her father to forgive her and to at least send her a bit of clothing. "...almost naked, no shoes nor stockings to wear."

Here, within these pages, the mystery of Elizabeth Sprigs is revealed. It is a tale based on a single letter sent from Baltimore so long ago.

Now available at Amazon, Apple, Nook, Kobo and other online retailers in print and digital editions!

JENNIE WADE:
A GIRL FROM GETTYSBURG

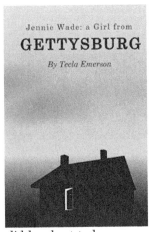

It had been foolish to stay but now there was no choice. It was anyone's guess what the outcome would be. Nothing was as it should be. Oddly, the Confederate troops were pouring in from the north and Union troops were marching in from the south. They arrived in droves. The town was not prepared for what happened during the early days of the summer, 1863. Jennie, a young local girl, did her best to keep up with the demand for bread and water and medical care for the troops. Her brothers were scattered, her sister would soon be having a baby, her mother was not bearing up well and Jack, her intended, had not been heard from in weeks. It was a time and place that would be recorded in American history forever. A time marked by the largest number of casualties in the Civil War. It was Gettysburg, Pennsylvania, a small, unremarkable town; an easily forgotten town that would live in infamy and one that history would never forget. Of the almost 50,000 casualties of that encounter in early July, only one civilian was killed. This is her story. The story of Jennie Wade, a dedicated young woman thrown into the middle of one of Americans' most tragic times.

Now available at Amazon, Apple, Nook, Kobo and other online retailers in print and digital editions!

Printed in Great Britain
by Amazon